Ted Hughes was born in 1930. He is the author of numerous collections of poems and books for children, as well as critical studies of Shakespeare and T. S. Eliot and a volume of occasional prose entitled *Winter Pollen* (1994). His *New Selected Poems 1957–1994* appeared in 1995. In 1984 he was appointed Poet Laureate.

Difficulties
of a Bridegroom

TED HUGHES

faber and faber

First published in 1995
by Faber and Faber Limited
3 Queen Square London WC1N 3AU
This paperback edition first published in 1996

Phototypeset by Wilmaset Ltd, Wirral
Printed and bound in Great Britain by
Mackays of Chatham PLC, Chatham, Kent

A CIP record for this book
is available from the British Library

ISBN 0–571–17482–5

2 4 6 8 10 9 7 5 3 1

Contents

Foreword

These nine pieces hang together, in my own mind, as an accompaniment to my poems. The fable 'O'Kelly's Angel' came first, written during the year I left University (1954), as a joke of sorts about Terence McCaughey, my closest friend through those college years, who did later become, just as in my story, a professor (of Ancient Irish) at Trinity College, Dublin. The point of the joke was to put a Protestant – Presbyterian – Ulsterman at the head of a Catholic Fundamentalist army. (In those days the troubles of Northern Ireland were dormant.) I kept the piece, with all its naiveties, mainly because I could not forget it, and occasionally thought of tackling it in some more serious form – till history overtook it.

'Snow' came next, late 1956.

'Sunday' came next in 1957, as one of a planned series of autobiographical stories about my boyhood in Yorkshire. The plan disintegrated, but 'Sunday' and two more stories, 'The Rain Horse' and 'The Harvesting', which followed in that order during 1958–9, use that source of material. The *Observer* newspaper held a competition for a short story titled 'The Return'. 'The Rain-Horse' was to be my entry, but the writing dragged me in and the deadline passed. Both these stories are set on a farm in South Yorkshire which was my constant playground between 1938 and about 1944. The poetic centre of gravity of these five pieces passes from the caged angel to the other-life other-world of snow, to the caged and helpless rat, to the domineering horse, to the hare that the protagonist becomes at the moment of its death.

'The Wound' came next, in 1961. For two or three months that spring I was absorbed in making an oratorio of the *Bardo Thodol* – the Tibetan *Book of the Dead* – for the American/Chinese composer Chou Wen Chung. My completion of my first draft coincided with a peculiar dream. This dream took the form of a full-length film, about an episode in the Second World War, with myself in one of the parts (Ripley). It was accompanied by an epic/dramatic parallel text, as subtitles, in a kind of verse. I woke from the dream with the understanding that both film and text had been composed by John Arden (whose play, *Sergeant Musgrave's Dance*, was in the news at the time). I was mortified to see something so intimately my own pre-empted by somebody else. Waking further, I realized that of course it was my own. I then went back to sleep and re-dreamed the whole thing, every scene and line identical to the first performance. Waking from this second session I understood, absolutely, that it was my Gothic/Celtic version of the *Bardo Thodol* – the journey of the soul in the forty-nine days after death, ending in rebirth. On this occasion my person from Porlock was an appointment to go with a friend to watch a case at the Old Bailey. Before I left, I made a few notes about the dream – confident that I could never forget one frame or word of something so vividly fixed in my memory. But by the time I got back the whole verbal text had gone, except for a few odd phrases. I adapted the film to a radio play, cutting out many of the scenes, and titled it 'The Wound'.

A year later I wrote 'The Suitor' over the two days and nights before, during and after the birth of my son. At the time I saw it as an exercise, an attempt to find the concentration of tone that

I associate with John Carlyle's prose translation of *The Divine Comedy*. When I showed it to Ben Sonnenberg (who started and edited *Grand Street*) later on, he remarked: 'You should have called it "Death and the Maiden".'

Some time around 1962, I hit on the phrase 'Difficulties of a Bridegroom' and this became the working title of almost everything I wrote for the next few years. I tried to explore the theme with various small plays and prose scenarios, and with one *Peer Gynt*-style unending succession of alchemical scenes in verse. None of this struck me as very satisfactory. Then for compelling reasons I deliberately stopped trying to write stories or plays. Several pieces that I had already drafted I abandoned. Only one of these survived. Written as a film scenario in 1962–3, I rewrote it much later (in 1975), in rough verse and abbreviated form, simply to lay claim to the sequence of situations which by that time, it seemed to me, were beginning to leak out into other people's books. It was published as *Gaudete,* in which the lives of the two Reverend Lumbs are shaped by my hidden title. Meanwhile two collections of verse, *Crow* and *Cave Birds*, grew from the same preoccupation.

In 1978, Emma Tennant asked me for a 'fairy story' for her magazine *Bananas*, and I wrote 'The Head'. Later on it occurred to me that this was one form of the closing chapter, a metaphor for the successful final event, of my alchemical title.

Then recently, in 1993, Michael Morpurgo asked me for a ghost story, perhaps suitable for children, to be part of an anthology of ghost stories set in various locations belonging to the National Trust. By chance, an early experience of my own filled the requirements, and I wrote it out, with a few adjustments to what I remember, as 'The Deadfall'. After I had finished this I saw, as anybody might, just how it formed the natural overture to the sequence of which 'The Head' is the finale.

The Deadfall

I own a tiny ivory fox about an inch and a half long. Most likely an Eskimo carving. It came to me in one of the strangest incidents of my life.

My mother saw ghosts, now and again. Different kinds. One night during the last war she woke, feeling dreadfully agitated. She lay for a while, feeling more and more agitated. At last she got out of bed and, opening the curtains, saw an amazing sight. Across the street stood St George's Church. And above the church, the whole sky was throbbing with flashing crosses. As she told of it next day, there were thousands on thousands, flashing and fading, in and out, the whole sky covered with them, coming very thick, like big snowflakes hitting and breaking and melting on a warm window. She tried to wake my father. 'There's the most terrible battle somewhere,' she told him. 'Thousands of boys are being killed.' He heard what she said, but he wouldn't be roused. He had to get up at five a.m. anyway, as every morning. She went back to the window and watched for a long time, going to bed finally only when she got too cold.

Next day, the radio announced that the British and American armies had landed that night in Northern France, and were fighting their way inland through the German defences.

Another time, she was awakened by a sickening pain across

1

the back of her neck and a terrific banging. Short, urgent bursts of banging, as if somebody were pounding hard on a door or hammering on a table. She couldn't tell where the noise came from. 'It shook this house,' she said. Again she got up and looked out of the window. But the street, which was the main street of the town, was deserted. She went downstairs, made herself a cup of tea, and sat with the pain. It felt, she said, like toothache – but in her neck. She couldn't tell how the banging stopped – eventually it just wasn't there any more. But she still had the pain next morning when the telegram came with the news of the violent death, during the night, of one of her brothers.

She was ready for this news. She had known somebody in her family was going to die. And the moment she read the telegram the pain went.

Another time, while she was pushing a Hoover around the sitting-room, mid-afternoon, her eldest brother walked in. She was alarmed, since she knew that he was actually lying unable to move in Halifax hospital. As she switched off the Hoover to speak to him, he faded. She noted the time, guessing he had died that very moment. Again, she had known that one of her family was going to die.

Each time, she was warned in the same way. Among her seven or eight brothers and sisters, as a girl her closest friend had been the sister closest to her in age, Miriam. This sister died when both were in their late teens. A few months after her death, Miriam reappeared at night and sat on my mother's bed, just as in life, and held her hand. Without speaking, she seemed to be consoling my mother. Two days later, their baby brother died.

After that, through the years, just before any member of her family died, Miriam would appear at my mother's bedside. But as the years passed, her ghost changed. She became brighter

2

and taller. 'Gradually,' said my mother, 'she has turned into an angel.' By the time of that last occasion, when their eldest brother died, Miriam had become a tall glowing angel with folded wings. My mother described her as being made of flame. As if she were covered with many-coloured feathers of soft, pouring flame. But it was still Miriam. And on this last visit, as she stood by the bed, my mother reached up a hand to stroke the flame because it was, as she said, 'so beautiful', 'The feel of it,' she told us afterwards, 'was like the taste of honey.' I remember her telling that, the next day, as if it were only minutes ago.

My brother and sister and I also wanted to see ghosts.

We lived near Hebden Bridge, in West Yorkshire, in a village called Mytholmroyd. There the river runs in a deep valley, under high horizons of empty moorland. On one side of that valley, in a steep wood of oak and birch trees, is an ancient grave. At least, it was always known as a grave. We called it the grave of the ancient Briton. A great rough slab of stone. My brother, much older than me, sometimes tried to dig him up, with the help of a few friends. I remember scraping away there, on two or three occasions. The stone was embedded in a hole and far too big for us to lever out. We tried to dig round it and under it. But the great slab simply settled deeper.

My brother liked to camp out on the hillsides, and would take me with him. Once, when he and I were camping down by the stream, in that wood, not far from the grave, he got the idea of raising the ancient Briton's ghost.

He must have already thought about it quite carefully, because he was prepared. Perhaps not very well prepared. He had brought half a bottle of sweet wine made from black-berries. One of our uncles concocted that sort of thing. This was to work the magic trick.

He woke me in the middle of the night. I pulled on my boots

and climbed through the woods behind him. I liked being in the woods at night, but by the time we got to the grave I was nervous. I remember I didn't want him to go too near the grave. I thought something might grab him and pull him in. Then I would be alone, in a dark wood, with my brother somewhere beneath me being dragged deeper into the earth. I didn't like that idea.

He had already made what he called the altar – a flat piece of stone near the grave's edge. Now he lit a fire over this stone. I saw he had firewood ready. In his preparations he had even emptied the charge out of some twelve-bore cartridges, to make sure he got an instant flare-up blaze, by lighting the loose explosive. That was a success. It lit up the tree trunks and the over-curving boughs in a great woosh of light, as if they'd flung up their arms. Then it settled down to burn the twigs and sticks he'd piled in a wigwam shape. He was an expert firemaker and in no time had a good blaze going.

Now he stood up with his bottle of wine and carefully tipped it, letting a trickle spatter into the flames. The glow blackened and hissed, as a pale cloud billowed up. He began to speak:

'O Ancient Briton, I am pouring out this redness to give life to you. Rise up, O Ancient Briton, all this is for you. Rise up and warm yourself. Rise up, O Ancient Briton, and quench your ancient thirst.'

I remember that 'quench your ancient thirst', because that was the first time I ever felt the sensation of my hair freezing solid, like a cap of ice. And I was suddenly afraid. I could see the Ancient Briton, deep in the earth, with his corpse teeth bared. Probably his eyes had just flown open. I just knew he would come – and we wouldn't know what to do about it. What could my brother do, when that thing started walking towards us?

My brother was already backing towards me, as if he'd seen

4

something down there in the pit where the stone lay. As he came, he was still trickling wine out on to the tough, leathery grass of the wood. Then he set the bottle down, propped at an angle, still with some wine in it, half way between me and the fire, and joined me. The fire had recovered, the blackberry wine seemed to have helped it.

Perhaps he did other things that I hadn't noticed. We watched the flames and the huge caves of blackness between the tree trunks. Little sparks went writhing up in the reddened smoke. I stared hard, to see a shape beyond them. I kept an eye on the bottle.

I expected something. Maybe a dark lump like an animal would heave itself up out of the hole. Or maybe a person would somehow be there, standing beside the grave, looking towards us.

Or maybe we wouldn't see anything, but the bottle would suddenly rise up in the air and tilt, as an invisible mouth drank at it. Then a shape would grow solid between us and the fire, with the bottle in its hand.

But the worst thought was, if something did come, what would we do?

We crouched there, watching the fire till the flames died.

I asked in a whisper if he thought we should go back to the tent, but he hissed so sharp and tense I felt the hair prickle all over my body. He was staring towards the glow of the fire's embers. I tried to see what he was looking at.

'I thought I saw something,' he whispered.

I began to hear sounds in the wood, rustling and tickings. I felt sleepy. Surely the fire had gone out now. He got up at last and walked over to it. I followed him, to stay close. He picked up the bottle, and poured the last drops on to the fire's remains. He turned the altar over with his foot. Nothing had happened.

*

My little ivory fox came the following summer. This time we were camping in the valley known as Crimsworth Dene.

Our father and mother had both been born in Hebden Bridge. Their paradise had been the deep, cliffy, dead-end gorge of Hardcastle Crags, which cuts back north-west into the moors from Hebden Bridge, full of trees, with a rocky river. The big old mill building still standing there, well up the gorge, was used as a dance-hall in those days, where all the boys and girls of Hebden Bridge did their courting. Nowadays, this place is a famous beauty spot. More than once, people from Hebden Bridge, on holiday in Blackpool or Morecambe, have purchased a bus ticket for a day's mystery tour to a beauty spot, and have been brought back to Hardcastle Crags.

Crimsworth Dene is a more secret valley that forks away due north, from the bottom of Hardcastle Crags.

Like all these valleys, Crimsworth Dene is steep-sided, deep, with woods overhanging stone-walled falling-away fields. And above the woods, more stone-walled fields, climbing to a farm or two. And above the farms the moors – the empty prairies of heather that roll away north into Scotland. And in the very bottom of the valley, the dark, deep cleft, thick with beech, oak, sycamore, plunging to an invisible stream.

On the west slope, an old stony packhorse road clambers north between dry-stone walls, under the hanging woods and above the lower fields, finally up and out across the moor towards Haworth. About a mile up that road, on the left, under the trees and over the roadway, is a little level clearing.

Perhaps it was once a quarry, for the stone of the local walls. Here, when they were boys, before the First World War, my mother's brothers used to camp. They called Crimsworth Dene 'the happy valley'. The strangest thing that ever happened to me happened there.

One week, my brother decided to camp there. Though it

was right in the heart of the territory that belonged, as I felt, to our mother and father, it was a little outside ours. But our uncles knew the farmers, and they had given my brother permission to shoot rabbits and magpies and such like. Now and again he did roam this far with his rifle, but only rarely and briefly. For me, though I had always known Hardcastle Crags, it was the first time I had ever entered Crimsworth Dene. I was still quite young, only seven.

As we pitched our tent on the Friday evening, on that little clearing, under the trees, I knew this was the most magical place I had ever been in. The air was very still, and the sky clear after a warm day. All down the valley, over the great spilling mounds of foxgloves, grey columns of midges hung in the stillness, like vertical smoke above camp-fires. I brought water up from the stream in our rope-handled canvas bucket, and collected dead sticks for firewood, while he sorted our bedding, the pans and cutlery, and made a fireplace with stones. All the while a bird sang on the very topmost twig of a tree over the clearing. I had never heard a bird like it, nor have I since.

It was a thrush, I expect. But every note echoed through the whole valley. I felt I had to talk in whispers. Even so, I thought each word we spoke would be heard in Pecket, away out of sight round the hill's shoulder, a mile or more away.

My brother got a fire going and warmed up our beans. Camping is mainly about camp-fires, food cooked on camp-fires, and going to sleep in a tent. And getting up in the wet dawn. We planned to get up at dawn, maybe before dawn, when the rabbits would be dopey, bobbing about in the long dewy grass. Our precious, beautiful thing, my brother's gleaming American rifle, lay in the tent, on a blanket.

As it grew dark, I kept hearing a tune in my head and the words of the song. It came to me whenever I looked down over the deep grass of the steep field below us towards that plunge of dark trees. Very clear I heard:

> If you go down to the woods today
> You're sure of a big surprise

and the strange tune of that song, which sounds like a bear romping through a gloomy forest.

As I lay on my groundsheet, under my blanket at last, looking up at the taut canvas of our ex-army bell-tent, and listening to the stars, and the huge, silent breathing of the valley, I felt happier than I had ever been. And wider awake than I had ever been. Even so, I went straight off to sleep.

I woke in the dark, thinking it must be time to get up. I lay listening for night creatures. After a long time I began to hear cock-crows, then the tent walls began to pale. My brother woke and, without breakfast, we were off.

Dark tracks of rabbits were everywhere in the white of the heavy dew. I looked at the tracks quite close around our tent. Why hadn't I heard whatever made them? What had made them? Rabbits, or something else?

Usually, one rabbit was all we could expect to shoot. But because this was new hunting ground, and because the place seemed so magically wild, secret and undisturbed, I was hoping for a record bag. We saw hardly a rabbit. Only the odd white tail far off, just glimpsed then gone. The sun rose. The dew glittered and dried. We tramped all over the hillside, up as far as the moor. We skulked along the edges of woods, peering over walls. We had to inspect every tiny thing. It might be a snipe. Or the lifted head of a grouse strayed down off the high ground. But my brother did not fire one shot. For the last part of the morning we stretched out in the heather and he sunbathed.

But then, coming back to our camp for breakfast at midday,

we found something curious. The wall along the top of the wood, directly above our camp, had a tumbledown gap. As we came down through that gap, my brother pointed.

Under the wall, on the wood side, a big flat stone like a flagstone, big as a big gravestone, leaned outwards, on end. It was supported, I saw, by a man-made contraption of slender sticks. Tucked in behind the sticks, under the leaning slab, lay a dead wood pigeon, its breast torn, showing the dark meat.

'Gamekeeper's deadfall,' said my brother.

It was the first deadfall I had seen set. I had read about them, made of massive tree trunks, used by trappers in the Canadian forests for bears, wolves, wolverines. My brother explained how it worked. How one light touch on the tripstick would collapse the support and bring the great stone slam down flat – on top of whatever was under it.

I went past it warily. I didn't want the jolt of my tread to bring it down.

'The pigeon is fresh,' said my brother. 'He must have baited it yesterday. Or maybe this morning. For a fox, probably.'

We hadn't seen the gamekeeper, who looked after Lord Savile's grouse up on the moor. He only became a danger if you'd shot some of his grouse and this time we hadn't. Still, we'd kept a sharp lookout for him.

A gamekeeper usually sees you first. And the moment he sees you, he becomes invisible – until he's right on top of you.

In the afternoon, we went back up on to the heather. My brother was mad about sunbathing. He rubbed himself with olive oil and lay there frying. I lay for a while. But I wasn't mad about the sun. I left that to him. Eventually, I found a trickle of water that overflowed an old drinking trough and spent the afternoon making dams and channels.

Rabbits usually come out again about four o'clock. But still we had no luck. Somehow, in spite of all those tracks in the early dew, and in spite of the silent, lonely emptiness of the valley, rabbits seemed to know better than to show themselves in the day. We ended up drinking tea at a farmhouse, where the farmer said his old mother, who made the tea, then sat watching us from a rocking chair in the corner, was some remote cousin of our grandmother. After that, he wanted us to shoot a particular rat. This rat was stealing eggs, according to him. Its front doorway was a crevice under the threshold of an old stable. Every evening he saw it. But it was far too smart to be trapped. He gave us two addled eggs that we propped up, very visible, three yards in front of its hole. Then we climbed to a hayloft, and lay looking down at both eggs and rat-hole, through the open loft-door.

We lay there unmoving, on the warm boards, with our eyes on that hole, till the light began to fail. Maybe the rat was watching us from inside his hole. He never appeared. I became impatient, thinking of the rabbits we were missing. They were probably out all over the place. I wanted to take home at least one.

Finally, my brother gave in and we went back down over the fields from the high farm, to our camp. We saw rabbits, but it was too dark now to see the sights of the rifle. Anyway, I found I was more interested in getting to the gap in the wall. I couldn't wait to see the trap. I imagined a great red fox in it, squashed flat. Or maybe a stoat. A stoat would easily trip those frail, balanced sticks. Or maybe even a crow. A stoat might leap clear.

But it yawned there just as we'd left it, and the wood pigeon lay untouched.

My idea of the valley was changing. I had thought of it teeming with stoats, weasels, foxes – as well as rabbits. But here, as everywhere else, perhaps the gamekeepers and the poultry farmers were in control. Even crows. I hadn't seen a

crow. I hadn't seen a magpie. A magpie would have found that
wood pigeon anywhere in the valley.

But the gamekeeper had set the trap, so there must be
something. Maybe as my brother said there was a fox. A
lone fox, a notorious, solitary bandit, with his hide-out in
this wood, near our camp. Among rocks, maybe, where
he couldn't be dug out. And maybe tomorrow morning he'd
be there, flat under the fallen slab. Or she. It might be a
vixen.

The evening was as still as the night before. As we fried eggs
and bacon, and our pork and beans to go with them, the
magical spell came over me again. The thought of a fox very
near, deep in his den, maybe smelling our bacon, made
everything more mysterious. I kept looking down through the
dusk into the crevasse of dark trees below, to give myself the
eerie feeling of that tune again, and the strange words:

> If you go down to the woods today
> You're sure of a big surprise

It never failed. As the valley grew darker, the feeling, with
its bear coming up through the forest, grew even stronger. I
found that whenever I looked down there and thought of that
tune, I could make myself shiver and freeze. I could do it again
and again, first looking away then looking back down there
and hearing the tune. Each time I would shiver and freeze
afresh. I kept testing myself to see if it would go on happening.
Like touching myself with an electric spark. And every time it
happened.

The fox would be smelling our bacon all right, and our
coffee. We always brewed coffee in the dusk. That was the part
I liked best of all, sitting there, gazing into the fire and sipping
sweet, scalding coffee, while the thick sticks crumbled to a
cave of glow, whitening the hearthstones. Maybe those tracks

in the dew last night had been the fox, inspecting us and our fireplace and looking for leftovers.

Again we planned to get up early. Some time tomorrow, Sunday, we would have to set off back home. My brother wanted to bag something as badly as I did. He was regretting wasting time on the rat.

That night I tried to stay awake, so I could have every minute of lying there under my blanket, listening. Each tiny sound had to be something. I could hear the stream, down in the bottom. Why hadn't I heard that the night before? Would I hear a fox if he came right up to the tent wall, and sniffed at me through the canvas?

At some point I drifted off to sleep because when I woke I thought it was dawn. Then I realized, the pale light coming through the canvas was moonlight. I was absolutely alert, and tense. Something had wakened me. I lay there, hardly daring to breathe. Then I heard a whisper, a low hiss of a whisper, outside the tent. It was calling my name.

Somebody was out there.

Beside me, fast asleep, my brother was breathing gently. I simply listened. I don't know what I thought. I felt no fear, but still I was amazed to feel the tears trickling slowly down over my ears, as I lay staring upwards.

The whisper came again, my name. It seemed to be coming from about where the fire was.

Very carefully, partly not to waken my brother, partly not to let the voice know I was listening, I sat up, leaned forward, and tried to peep through the laced-up door of the tent. By holding the edges of the flaps slightly open, I could see a tiny dot of red glow still in our fireplace. Everything out there was drenched in a grey, misty light.

Somebody was standing beside the fireplace.

The Deadfall

It was a person and yet I got the impression it was somehow
not a person. Or it was a very small person. It looked like a
small old woman, with a peculiar bonnet on her head and a
long shawl. That was my impression. As I stared with all my
might, trying to make out something definite, this figure
drifted backwards into the shade of the trees. But the whisper
came again:

'Come out. Quickly. There's been an accident.'

I immediately knew it must be somebody from the farm.
Surely it was the farmer's little old mother. That was how she
knew we were here. The farmer had fallen down a well, or
down a loft ladder, or a mad, calving cow had gored him and
crushed his ribs. Or he'd simply tumbled downstairs going to
get his old mother a cup of tea because she couldn't sleep.

Something stopped me waking my brother. What I really
wanted was to find out more. Who was this person? What was
the accident? Anyway, it was my name that had been called. It
must be me that was specially needed. I could come back and
tell my brother later. Most of all, I wanted to see who this was.

I had gone to sleep in my clothes, to keep warm and for a
quick start. So now I pulled on my boots. I unlaced the tent
door at the bottom and crawled out. The grass was cold and
soaking under my hands.

'Hurry,' came the whisper from the trees. 'Hurry, hurry.'

It seems strange, that I felt no fear. I was so sure that it was
somebody from the farm, that I thought of no other possibility.
Only huge curiosity, and excitement. Also, I felt quite import-
ant suddenly.

I went towards the voice, staring into the dark shade. The
moon was past full but very hard and white. I wanted to get
into the shade quickly, where I wouldn't be so visible.

But now the voice came again, from further up the wood.
Yes, the voice was climbing towards the farm.

13

'Hurry,' it kept saying. 'Hurry up.'

Beneath the trees, the slope was clear and grassy, without brambles or undergrowth. Easy going but steep, with that tough, slippery grass.

As I climbed, the voice went ahead. Very soon, I could see through the top of the wood. The bright night sky was piled with brilliant masses of snowy cloud, beyond the dark tree stems. I glimpsed the black silhouette now and again, the funny bonnet, climbing ahead, bobbing between the trees.

'Are you coming?' came the whisper again. 'This way.'

I saw her shape in the gap of the wall, clear against those snowy clouds. Then she had gone through it. It was now, as I came up towards the gap, sometimes grasping tussocks to help myself upwards, that I saw something else, bouncing and scrabbling under the wall in a clear patch of moonlight.

At first I thought it was a rabbit, just this moment scared into a snare by our approach, now leaping and flinging itself to be free, but tethered by the pegged snare. It was the size of a rabbit. Then I smelt the rich, powerful smell.

With a shock, I remembered. I had come right up to the deadfall.

The great slab of stone had fallen. Beside it sat a well-grown fox cub, staring up at me, panting. As I took this in, the cub suddenly started again, tugging and bouncing, jerking and scrabbling, without a sound, till again it crouched there, staring up at me, its mouth wide open, its tongue dangling, panting.

I could see now that it was trapped by one hind leg and its tail. They were pinned to the ground under the corner of the big slab.

The smell was overpowering, thick, choking, almost liquid, as if concentrated liquid scent had been poured over me, saturating my clothes and hands. I knew the smell of fox – the overpowering smell of frightened fox.

14

Then I looked up and saw the figure out there in the field, only five yards away, watching me. More than ever I could see it was a little old woman, with her very thin legs and her funny bonnet and shawl. She did not seem to be wanting me to go to the farm. She had brought me to this fox cub. She was probably some eccentric old lady who never slept, or slept only by day and spent the night roaming the hillsides, talking to owls and befriending foxes. She would have seen our camp. Probably some of those tracks had been hers, brushed through the dew around our tent. Now she had found the trapped cub, and not being strong enough to lift the slab, she had come to us. She wanted me to lift the slab and free the cub. She had not called my brother because she thought he might kill it. She must have watched us, and heard him speak my name.

My first thought was to catch the cub and keep it alive. But how could I hold it and at the same time lift the slab? It was a desperate, ferocious little thing. I could have wrapped it in my jersey, knotting the arms around it. But I didn't think of that. As I put my fingers under the other corner of the slab, the cub snapped its teeth at me and hissed like a cat, then struggled again, jerking to free itself.

With all my strength I was just able to budge the slab a fraction. But it was enough. As the slab shifted, the cub scrabbled and was gone – off down the wood like a rocket.

I looked up at the old lady, and this was my next surprise. The bare, close-cropped, moonlit field was empty. I walked out to where she had been. The whole wide field, under the great bare sky of moonlight, all made much brighter by that bulging heap of snowy, silvery clouds, was empty. Not even a sheep. Absolutely nothing.

She couldn't have run away. I had looked down for only a few seconds. She had simply gone. I could see every blade of grass where she had stood. The field wall. The trees of the wood. The hilltops above and beyond.

I came back to the deadfall. Now I saw that it lay at a slight tilt. There was something beneath it. Another cub, maybe. I tried again to lift it. But I still could not budge it more than that quarter inch, and only for a second. I could not possibly lift it.

It was as I came back down to our campsite that I saw somebody standing outside the tent, in the moonlight. I stopped, hidden under the trees. With a sudden terrible thought, I remembered the Ancient Briton. And now, for the first time, I really was frightened.

But then I heard my name called in a familiar low voice. It was my brother. He had come out of the tent. And now he had heard me.

'Where have you been?'

I told him what had happened. All he said was, 'We'll have a look in the morning. Come and get back to sleep.'

But I lay awake. The tent darkened and became pitch black. Either the moon had gone down or that cloud had come up and covered it. Then I heard the prickling sound of light rain on the canvas.

The rain grew heavier, and soon it was filling the whole world, like a steady tearing of canvas inside my head. A drop hit my face.

Slowly the canvas paled. I heard cocks crowing in the high farms and dozed off. Next thing I smelt bacon. The rain had stopped. It was day.

'Come on, let's eat everything,' called my brother.

I wanted to see the deadfall, but he would not be hurried. We scoured our pans and dishes with grit and water and bundled them into their bag. He began to take down the wet tent. In a few minutes everything was inside the bulging kitbag. The rain had come back by now, but more of a drizzle.

It looked to be setting in for the day. The shooting trip was over, I could see.

But now he took his rifle from under the tree where he'd leaned it in the dry with the bag over its muzzle, and started off up the wood.

The deadfall lay as I had left it. He handed the rifle to me, put his fingers under the slab and heaved it back against the wall. There, at our feet, lay a big red fox, quite dead, the wood pigeon still in its mouth.

He pulled it clear and inspected it. The body was stiff. He picked it up by one hind leg. A foreleg stuck out at an angle. Its head was twisted to one side, keeping its grip on the dead bird. Only the tail plumed over, like a fern. I had expected to see whatever was under there flattened like a rat on the road. It did look slightly flattened, its fur was flattened.

Still carrying the dead animal by the one hind leg, my brother took the rifle from me and started off down the wood. But then he turned back, handed me the rifle again, and pulled the deadfall slab over. It dropped with a shocking thud into its position. I felt the earth bounce.

'This fox escaped,' he said.

Down at our campsite, he brought out our little axe. I asked him what we were going to do with the fox. Wasn't it the gamekeeper's? I remember his answer:

'This fox belongs to itself.'

Then he began to dig a hole with the axe in the middle of the patch of grass flattened by our tent. He cut out the turf and set it aside, then hacked downwards, scooping the loosened soil out with his hands, till he began to hit stones. The hole was about two feet deep. He jabbed about down there with a sharpened stick, dislodging stones, and shaping the bottom of the hole. I crouched beside the work, watching the hole and looking at the fox. I had never examined a fox. It was so astonishing to see it there, so real, so near. When I lifted its eyelid, the eye looked at me, very bright and alive. I closed it gently and stroked it quite shut. Its face was slightly squashed-looking, but with no visible damage, no blood. And so peculiar, with the wood pigeon gripped in its mouth.

My brother picked it up again.

'Do you want its tail?' he asked me. I shook my head.

He fitted it neatly into the bottom of the hole, and arranged it, bending the stiff, jutting foreleg to look more comfortable. We tucked the little stones around it, and covered it with the gritty black soil. Then the turfs. He took out some of the soil and threw it away, to let the turfs lie flat. I helped him push loose soil out of sight down between the sliced turfs. As I was doing this, I felt a knobbly pebble and saw under my fingers what looked like one of those white quartz pebbles you find embedded in the black boulders on the moor. But then I realized it was not a pebble.

I stood up to examine it. I could not believe what I had in my hand. It was this little ivory fox. I was so startled that I simply gripped it. Maybe I thought my brother might take it off me.

'What's wrong?' he asked, looking up. He never missed anything. But I managed to shift my inspection to the back of my fingers. I got my find into my pocket and bent again to the grave. He was combing the grass of the turfs with his fingers, drawing it over the edges, to make it look like unbroken sod again.

When he'd finished, you couldn't really tell it was there, even from quite close. Everything looked like the scuffed and trampled patch where a tent has been. As I stood there, I could feel him watching me. 'Are you all right?' he asked.

We had to walk down to Hebden Bridge, in the drizzle, to catch a bus home. He carried the kit bag. I carried the rifle. He had not fired one shot.

The Deadfall

It was while we were waiting at the bus stop that he asked me who I thought the old woman was last night. Well, I said, it must have been just some old woman.

'But you said she vanished.'

'She did. One second she was there, and the next she wasn't.'

'Do you think,' he said, 'it might have been the dead fox's ghost?'

So it was there, standing at the bus stop in Hebden Bridge, that I first had to wonder whether I had seen a ghost. I didn't know what to think about it. But two or three times since then I have seen what seemed to be a ghost, and I know that as soon as the moment's passed – you don't know what to think about it. I didn't know what to think about the little ivory fox either – the fox in my pocket. Who could have dropped it where I found it? One of our uncles long ago? Obviously, when a thing's dropped like that it doesn't vanish into the never never. It has to stay right there. So this fox could have been there long before our uncles. Long, long, long before. Like the stones. What made me feel slightly giddy was the way I'd found it while we were actually burying that fox. I did not know what to make of any of it. I could not see any way past it. When I thought about it, I felt a ring tightening round my head.

But there was the ivory fox in my pocket, so smooth and perfect. And after all these years, here it is, just as I found it. And I still do not know what to make of it. Or of that old lady either. If it was an old lady.

Later that year we moved away to another part of Yorkshire. I did not walk up Crimsworth Dene again, to look at the fox's grave, for many, many years.

19

O'Kelly's Angel

A FABLE

O'Kelly was a clerk in a government office. He was tired of his life. He had bigger ideas than would fit behind any desk.

One day, when he looked up to rest his eyes from the eight hundred and twelfth of a thousand forms in duplicate, he saw a wonderful thing. Usually, his only view – through a dirty window – was the dirty upper windows of the draper's store opposite. Today that view was changed. O'Kelly stared. His eyes popped, his red hair stood on end.

Hanging outside his window, directly above the street, was a blazing corona of about thirty angels.

O'Kelly got to the window as fast as he could. Seeing his face from the street, and not seeing what he was staring at, you would have thought he was some raving lunatic about to jump through the glass.

There was no doubt about it. They were angels. They were different sizes – between eight and fifteen feet high, shoulder to shoulder and facing outwards, their great eyes gazing steadily at nothing in this world. Their feet hung about twice the height of a man above the macadam. Fluttering rags of fire dropped from their down-pointing toes.

O'Kelly breathed deeply. He felt as though his heart might stop.

Then he noticed a curious thing.

One of the smallest angels was gradually moving out of formation. It was definitely drifting outwards, and slightly downwards, from its place in the corona.

O'Kelly saw his chance.

Two minutes later he stepped into the street, with a builder's rope, out of the office basement, coiled over his arm. By this time a dense crowd had collected. But under the angels the street was bare. Surrounding this arena, the people at the fore-edge of the crowd were leaning backwards, sometimes slipping or half falling, turning and scrambling, with fearful backward and upward looks at the blue conflagration suspended in the air.

As O'Kelly stepped into the deserted space, half the crowd gave a roar and half fell dead silent. Without a pause, he widened the noose at the end of the rope, and with an easy lift of his arm tossed it over the head of the separate angel. Then, gently, aware of the sudden complete silence of the crowd, he drew the noose as tight as gentleness could.

Now was the real test.

Bracing his feet wide apart, he took firm hold of the rope, and drew the angel towards him.

Would it put up a struggle? How strong is an angel? Would it rise, with a sudden thunder like a rocket, tearing his arms out?

The crowd gave a slow sigh.

Utterly without resistance, the angel came two clear yards out of formation.

Slowly, keeping his eyes fixed on his captive, ready to let go at the first sign of protest, O'Kelly backed up the street, and on either side of him the crowd fell away. At the same moment, as if their circuit had been broken, the other angels began to fade.

And as they faded they rose slowly. Out above the rooftops, for a while their forms glowed faintly against the low cloud. Then, quite suddenly, like a fading smudge of rainbow light, they were simply no longer anywhere. But nobody noticed. All eyes were fixed, like O'Kelly's, on that single, huge creature of soft flame, floating along there above him, following him so obediently.

Everything was going according to plan.

He tethered the angel in his garden, asked the police to keep the crowds out, and retired to the telephone.

The police had a hard time. All that night the crowd was thickening. The angel floated in a glow, like a brilliantly illumined kite, greening the leaves, high by the tops of the trees that bordered the garden.

By next morning, O'Kelly had everything he needed. A wheeled cage, such as circuses carry their tigers in, was brought to the garden gate. Within five minutes he had the angel inside it. His other purchase, a giant marquee, was being erected in the middle of Salisbury Plain, two hundred miles away.

The news of the angel had travelled fast and far. Over almost every radio on earth a special announcement had been made. Already, that morning, few papers were without a front-page mention of THE SIGN DIRECT FROM GOD, CAN IT BE FAKE? WHAT IS THE CHURCH GOING TO DO ABOUT THIS?, WILL THIS SAVE MANKIND?

Sometimes there was a whole column, the words of eye-witnesses in inverted commas. Sometimes there was an obscure photograph taken during the night – a shapeless flare-like effulgence high in the dark, above white upturned faces.

*

His journey to Salisbury was a national event.

The route was lined with crowds, as if for royalty. Whole towns had turned out, emptying their schools and factories on to the roadside.

Behind the cage came a dense, spectacular convoy. There were Daimlers, string-tied farmyard Fords, penny-farthings, brewers' drays loaded with brewers, removal vans crammed with removal men, buses bursting with conductors and drivers. There were tractors drawing wains loaded with yokels who had not stirred from their villages for forty years.

From all over England they were coming.

Along the route, every mile or so, a little band stood out from the roadside bearing banners with slogans: WELCOME TO THE EARTH, or, more passionately: SET US FREE.

The angel hung inside the cage, its attitude unchanged, soaringly erect, its toes six inches from the floor, its head within an inch of the ceiling, its eyes staring into nothing.

O'Kelly drove on steadily.

At three o'clock he reached the marquee. Salisbury Plain was a wonderful spectacle. O'Kelly had never seen so many cars. They were edged and inched cleverly into every fraction of spare ground. Farmers patrolled their fields, fighting and slowly losing a battle to keep their ploughland clear.

O'Kelly parked the cage in the middle of the marquee, and began to let the people in, fifty at a time, and each fifty for five minutes, to see the angel. He charged ten shillings per person. The men who had erected the marquee he now employed to control the crowd at the entrance, and to guard the cage.

The people were quiet.

'Once they realize this is a real angel, and no fake,' he said to himself, 'there'll be just no holding them. They'll walk through these tent walls like so much thin air. And what about the

23

police? And the church? Give me five days,' he prayed. 'Just five days. Then they can hang the thing in Canterbury cathedral for all I care.'

He took money till midnight, then closed the exhibition.

Next morning, at eight, showings began again. O'Kelly had never seen so much money in his life.

Nor so many people.

From the marquee entrance he could see nothing but people. A sea of heads. Here and there among them the gesticulating figures of lay preachers stood high on stools or boxes or car roofs, like dark angry towers. However the wind blew, it brought the sounds of Salvation Army brass bands and the hymning of choirs. All that second day the sight and sounds were the same.

And O'Kelly, noting the faces of the people who entered the marquee, saw their expressions change from scepticism or mere curiosity in the morning, to hushed, incredulous awe by nine o'clock that night.

In fact, the plain was the scene of an immense religious conversion.

And at the centre of it hung the angel, in a soft flame from head to foot, staring blankly, seeing nothing of its bars.

On the third morning the crowd was several million strong. The police, finding they could do nothing with it, watched it from the edge. Certain sections of the army were held in readiness. Not only from all over England, but from every country in the world, people were flocking to Salisbury. The Channel was like another Dunkirk, with little boats. The yachts, tankers and cargo boats of privateers plied busily across it, landing their loads of pilgrims on every point between Margate and Penzance. Private aircraft hung over the Atlantic like a collector's display. The customs gave up in despair.

Police helicopters flew over the crowd, ordering them through loudspeakers to disperse to their homes. But the crowd grew.

Then the police made an attempt to seal off the roads leading to the marquee, but the barriers were broken down, the police manhandled, and the crowd grew.

The queue to the entrance of the marquee was now over eight miles long. The main body of people just massed as near to the marquee as they could get, and camped.

To and fro in the crowd wound bands of hymn-singers, carrying banners: WE HAVE SEEN THE ANGEL OF THE LORD and FORSAKE YOUR EARTHLY TIES: WORSHIP THE LORD AND HIS ANGELS.

The lay preachers had never known such harvesting. Nor had there ever been such a crop of lay preachers.

'The angel proves beyond all last doubt that there is a God. The angel proves that there is a heaven. Therefore we must spend this life in earning that heaven. If there is a heaven, there is also a hell.'

The plain was becoming a vast revivalist meeting.

'This is more,' cried the self-appointed ministers of the new faith, 'than God has granted to any established church. The angel is the only true church.'

But over all this there was a sense of doom, a vivid atmosphere of foreboding.

IS THE ANGEL A WARNING OF THE PROMISED END?

The sentence was a big headline.

Talk of the angel filled all the newspapers. O'Kelly read these as closely as he observed his crowd. He marked just how opinions and sympathies swayed to and fro. At the first sign of danger he would be away.

But so far he seemed safe, massing his earnings. How long would this luck last?

It was evening. In the still summer air the sound of singing came from all over the plain – a continuous, low, undistinguished roar. The people filed past O'Kelly into the tent, with shining eyes, and kneeled, in silent rows, in front of the cage.

The angel hung, its attitude still unaltered, a flung tense uprightness, as though it were holding itself by pure intensity in the very tiptop of heaven. Its eyes stared beyond the world.

O'Kelly watched these worshippers. How long would it be now before the angel came to the end of its meditation? How soon would it bend its head forward, with an intense, unearthly, gathering roar of power, and burst out through the top of the marquee? Or when would it suddenly, without a sign, begin to fade and thin on the air, and disappear?

Next morning the newspapers brought O'Kelly news that made him stare. 'Massing of Roman Catholics to the north of Salisbury. The Pope remains silent.'

The rumour was that the Catholics were preparing to march on the marquee, capture the angel, and hang it in Saint Peter's at Rome. Some said it was the Pope's doing. 'The Pope's there in person,' they said, 'disguised.' Others said it was nothing but a rabble of Irishmen and unfrocked priests working themselves up for the rough-house of all time.

There was no telling where lies ended and truths began.

One thing was certain. The gathering was not of Irishmen only. True, every boat from Ireland was loaded with them, and Manchester, Liverpool and Glasgow were emptied of them. But in France, Italy and Spain, the people were rioting, striking, holding mass demonstrations, all demanding the angel for Rome. The governments were puzzled. While the Pope remained silent they dared do nothing. So the people took the matter into their own hands, and flocked towards England. Of all the French, Spaniards and Italians that landed every hour on the south coast, more than half ended up in the Catholic camp.

The spokesman was one McCaughey, a don from Trinity College, Dublin. He could orate like an electric drill, but all he would say to the press was: 'The angel for Rome.'

And he was certainly working his men up. Any Protestant venturing within a mile of their camp was as likely to be beaten senseless as not.

This gathering, known as the McCorkites, was already over a million strong. They lived in hotels, lodgings, buses, caravans, cars, tents, bothies, or in the open. And there was no likelihood of their dispersing either. The weather held good. Every night the Dog Star blazed brightly.

This was not all.

So far the Church of England had said nothing concerning the angel.

On the second day the two archbishops and several bishops had visited the marquee. First they had stared indignantly, then peered, then gone wide-eyed, then fallen on their knees. But whatever they had thought, they had said nothing, then, nor since.

Ordinary Anglican ministers were in a dilemma. They were constantly being badgered by their parishioners:

'Where does this angel fit in?'

And what could they say?

But now a spokesman had appeared. His name was Preston. He was a young, blond, energetic parson in Yorkshire. Wealthy American evangelists backed him from the start.

His attack was simple:

'This angel smacks of idolatry. And what if it is a miracle? Is

27

our faith so weak that we need a sign? Did not Christ rebuke the people when they demanded a sign? Is our faith to depend exclusively on what Christ openly despised?'

Then:

'This restraining of an Angel of the Lord in a cage, like a beast, with money taken for exhibition, as if it were a freak, is an insult against God and a shame on all mankind.'

In short, Preston meant to liberate the angel.

His supporters were swarming to Yorkshire, enduring any sort of roof or bed to be near him, ready for the 'Day of Liberation'.

When O'Kelly read all this he was furious.

'They are no more religious than I am,' he cried. 'They're just jealous of my initiative, jealous of my having got in first, jealous of my earning so much.'

He laughed. Or rather, he forced a laugh. That was a curious thing – he could no longer laugh. Lately his face had become fixed in a very strange expression – an uneasy mixture of horror and exhilaration, the face of a man who is wobbling on the last half of a tightrope over a canyon five miles deep. No matter how much he brushed his red hair, it was always sticking out on end in every direction. His mouth had set in a twist, slightly open. His eyes stared, with unnaturally arched wrinkles above them. When he looked in his shaving mirror, these eyes gave him a shock. And however he made his mouth smile shapes and wrinkled his cheeks, the eyes never altered.

The rest of the news was surprising enough.

Islam was confused. The angel was theirs, they had no doubt about it. They had sent mandates to the British Government stating that if the angel were not handed over at once, stronger measures would be taken to procure it.

From almost every country the British government had received a rebuke, that an Angel of the Lord should be permitted to remain in the hands of a commercial opportunist.

Besides this, in England, almost all industry was stopped for lack of men.

Reading on, O'Kelly wondered why the government didn't do something about it. But as he read the correspondence column, he realized why.

The marquee had become a second, greater Mecca. 'God is on Salisbury Plain, and O'Kelly will let you see him for ten shillings.' The words had gone round the world like a great shout. On Salisbury Plain was massed the touchiest, most single-minded force in the world.

They were already called 'The O'Kellians'.

When O'Kelly read this last, an idea came to him.

O'Kelly's idea was on a grand scale.

At huge cost, and within three days, he had a stadium erected. In the middle of the arena the marquee appeared like a tiny tent. It was the biggest stadium in the world.

O'Kelly now pulled the marquee down. In its place he suspended the angel, now in a kind of egg-shaped cage like a basket, above a high pulpit – a fine spectacle from every part of the auditorium. Then he let the place fill with O'Kellians, entrance free.

For the next hour, from the high pulpit, he gave sermons, and led hymn singing in a voice quite as fine as that of any of his lay preachers. He had a style with his preaching, too – any amount of glamorous passionate rant.

After half an hour a hundred of his men went among the congregation making a collection.

At this rate there were twelve services a day. And there was no doubt, the O'Kellians were the most solid, fervent church on earth, with O'Kelly their high priest.

And though he was pale and trembling from fatigue at the day's end, his income was multiplied times five.

By that eighth day O'Kelly was surprised at the way his angel had changed the world.

A new, fanatically honest dealing had made businessmen, for the most part, and even within so short a time, no richer than the rest. Prices had crashed. Thousands went bankrupt out of pure integrity, but were content.

Monasteries were crowded out. Schools and hostels were taken over to house the new monks. The deserts and wild places were every day more thickly populated with remorseful hermits. There was hardly a lonely road in the world without some haggard wretch on it, seeking a corner quiet enough to save his soul in.

On this same day there was a new excitement among the O'Kellians. The threat of the McCorkites and of the Prestonians was becoming oppressive. Disturbing conversations blew from the McCorkite camp:

'Wait till the French government – '

'And the Spanish – '

'And the Italian – '

'Come in with the armies,' some McCorkites had said.

'No, no,' others had cried, 'we must strike now.'

And from the Prestonian camp: 'A little more time – '

'Two days – '

'And the Archbishop of Canterbury will be in with us. Then the government will lend us the army.'

'No, no, we don't need it. Strike now.'

*

But worse than this, the rumours said, is the fearful way they are arming themselves.

'Arming themselves?' whispered the O'Kellians. And from thousands of parked cars around the stadium bits of metal began to vanish. At night, after the prayers and the hymns, O'Kelly could hear the filing and the tapping.

At last came the terrible ninth day.

As O'Kelly listened to the seven a.m. news on his little radio, he realized that the crisis had arrived. There were mass risings in Turkey and Greece. When the armies tried to quell these, they became violent. There was bloodshed. This spread to Italy, to France, to Spain.

O'Kelly sent his best lay preachers to lead the morning services, while he sat beside the radio, gnawing his thumb-nail.

At noon, after simmering all morning, an immense procession marched through Paris to throw out the indecisive government, bodily. They carried banners: THE ANGEL FOR ROME NOW. They were met by the army. There was a fearful massacre in Paris, and the rumour ran through France:

'The government's trying to stamp out religion – *écraser les pieux!*'

France rose. Thousands flocked to the airfields – '*À Salisbury! À Salisbury!*'

The fire ran into Italy and Spain. Dublin was one flame, and the glow and smoke in the sky visible from Anglesey. Nobody knew what horrors were going on under the horizon.

By two in the afternoon French, Italian and Spanish aircraft were dropping thousands of men, by parachute, hot from the fighting, on to the McCorkite camp. They were heavily armed and brought more arms. At three o'clock, from twelve miles north of Salisbury, the McCorkites began their march against O'Kelly.

Led by the same disastrous stars, Preston had that morning left Yorkshire with 317 long-distance coaches, all loaded with his men. Thousands more were making their own way to Salisbury, in lorries, in trains, in cars, on motorcycles. The 'Day of Liberation' had been well advertised.

Preston had made a last announcement:

'We have heard our rivals are armed. But I command you now, there shall be no violence. And after the angel is liberated, we shall fall on our knees, there in the very place of its violation, and pray.'

But the Prestonians had heard of the McCorkites. Under the bus seats were hatchets, rook-rifles, twelve-bores, Lugers looted during the war, bombs concocted in back kitchens, swords from the seventeenth century.

At four in the afternoon, the Prestonians mustered in Salisbury. With Preston at their head, singing martial hymns, holding their heads high, banners above them, they marched to music out on to the five mile road to the stadium.

When O'Kelly heard of this he ran, climbed into his car, and drove east, fast.

The O'Kellian camp included the whole of Salisbury. But four and a half miles from the stadium he met Preston's column. He drew up, at the side of the avenue which ran between parked blocks of O'Kellian cars, and watched the Prestonians pass.

First came Preston, his arms swinging high, his blond hair bright in the sun, the muscles of his face set like those of a bronze mask. He looked imperiously from side to side as he marched. The road was lined with O'Kellians wondering what they ought to do about this.

On either side of Preston strode a banner bearer. On one banner was the slogan: RENDER UNTO GOD THAT WHICH IS GOD's. On the other, simply: LIBERATE THE ANGEL

Then came over half a mile of ministers. They marched with determination, but not very happily. They could scarcely see for their own cloud of dust, and their sweating faces were grimed.

Behind the ministers came the main force. These made no pretence of marching in column. They filled the road, roaring indistinguishable hymns. O'Kelly saw rifles, shotguns, halberds.

And no end of banners:

'Don't let the Micks Get our Angel' and 'Down with the IRA' and 'The Angel For Ever' and 'Die for the Angel', 'The Angel is Ours', 'The Angel is God's'.

The column seemed endless.

Then, with two men staggering under it, O'Kelly saw a machine-gun.

He started the car, and nosed forward to a side lane. He felt definitely apprehensive. The rear of the Prestonian column, so far as he could see, was already nothing but a bloodthirsty mob. Where were the police?

He made a quick detour to the north, to reconnoitre the McCorkites. This was the first time he had penetrated the depths of the O'Kelly camp which stretched for a radius of five or six miles all around the stadium. The cars, caravans, tents and shanties were settled in square lots, with lanes between. Everywhere were food vans, water carts, rubbish wagons, sanitation carts, ice-cream vendors, tinkers, brewers' lorries, mobile laundries – O'Kelly weaved in and out, throwing up the dust. Far to his left he could see the dark bulk of the stadium.

He noticed there were no men in this part of the camp. Only women and children. And when he came on to the great North Way, down which the McCorkites must come, he found it eerily deserted. He drew up by a side lane.

All at once, over the north horizon, filling the road, came the McCorkite column.

O'Kelly felt his heart beating in his throat. Surely he wouldn't be recognized.

The column was led by McCaughey, who stood in a kind of howdah on top of a Guinness lorry. Other lorries followed at walking pace, loaded with priests. Then came the column on foot: at first many priests, then the laity. The first quarter mile of these were well enough, chanting piously, bearing rough crosses as in pictures of the early Christian martyrs.

The next mile was riotous. O'Kelly couldn't make out whether it was drunk or not. The first half mile was singing 'Kevin Barry' and 'The Boys of Wexford', one after the other, over and over. French, Spanish, Italians were there in plenty. There were rifles, swords, hedging bills, flintlocks, pitchforks, scythes, machine-guns.

And hundreds of banners. But only the one slogan:
THE ANGEL FOR ROME NOW.

O'Kelly turned off the main way and was back at the stadium within five minutes. Now he saw where the O'Kellian men were. The stadium was buried in a dense square of defenders. And the banner here, as far as he could see on every side, was:
THE ANGEL FOR THE WORLD.

They recognized him, and opened a lane. A minute later he was in his pulpit, in mid-service, ejecting the lay preacher in mid-hymn.

*

The O'Kellians had never known him so magnificent, and their throats responded. This, swore the survivors, was the finest service ever held, and well worth everything that followed. From the high pulpit O'Kelly kept watch on the two great main entrances, the south and the north.

Half an hour passed before he heard a hubbub to the south. Then, through the south door, he saw struggling in the crowd outside. He looked again to the north, and frowned. The defenders were quitting that part, obviously to reinforce the other. When he looked back to the south the spearpoint of Preston's column, Preston's blond head at the tip, had pierced the arena.

The hymn-singing collapsed into a thunderous roar as the congregation flowed down the steep tiers and thickened to take the brunt of Preston's thrust. An immense pushing contest followed. In the canyon of the southern entrance Preston's blond head danced like a cork in a harbour mouth. Beyond him, out on the plain, was a wild sea of strugglers.

Then a blow was struck.

That blow struck a spark in every man's brain there. Preston's head was still visible. 'Pax!' he was shouting. 'Pax!' Then a fist came up and he went down. From his high wonderful viewpoint, O'Kelly peered down. Certainly people were being trampled to death down there. But Preston re-appeared, and swung his fist.

His column, forced by the pressure from behind, was gradually piercing deeper, towards the pulpit and the angel.

'Pax!' roared O'Kelly through the loudspeakers. 'Pax!' he looked round him fearfully at the hasty skeleton structure of the stadium. He felt his pulpit tremble.

'The angel bids you be at peace!' he roared.

Above him, suspended on thin wires, the angel's cage hung like a beautiful lantern. The angel, as ever, burned high and erect within it, staring out over Salisbury Plain. Within its golden flame, blues and greens and dark reds came and faded, as if the fire of which it was made was itself on fire. It hung perfectly still.

'Stop them!' roared O'Kelly, looking up wildly, and pointing to the heaving arena.

But the angel stared on, and O'Kelly had to grab for a support as the pulpit rocked.

He glanced round at the northern entrance. That end of the stadium was emptied as the congregation crushed down to engage the Prestonians.

If the McCorkites should arrive now – !

A brewer's van charged through the northern entrance, piled with sword-waving, axe-waving figures – the McCorkite avant-garde. It was closely followed by three more lorries, loaded likewise. The McCorkites, seeing the battle in full swing, were wasting no time on negotiations. The O'Kellians turned to meet the threat, surrounded the lorries, and rushed on to man the north entrance, just in time to meet the head of the main McCorkite column.

That was how, at a little after five p.m., the battle started.

After five minutes, the first shot was fired.

After yet another five minutes, all O'Kelly could see was a terrible battlefield. From rim to rim the stadium heaved with struggling, hacking men. Dense smoke drifted over it from the plain outside where the Lord knows what desperate barricadoes and blazing cars were making their last gallant stands.

The machine-gunners fought each other from the opposite rims of the stadium, occasionally slicing a swath out of what they imagined to be the enemy ground forces. But by now the parties were so mingled it was hard to know who fought where. Except that the O'Kellians had formed a dense square of defenders around the pulpit. The McCorkites were striving to get in more men through the north entrance, and the O'Kellians outside the stadium were trying to stop them as they were trying to stop more Prestonians from forcing their way in through the south. At the same time those same O'Kellians from the outside of the stadium were struggling to break through in order to reinforce the main square that defended the pulpit, inside which O'Kelly crouched, sweating, under the still flame of the angel.

The machine-gun bullets cracked in the air above O'Kelly's head. He ducked down into the bottom of his pulpit and looked up at his angel. It hung, apparently unaware of the stray bullets that were chipping the cage bars.

Suddenly, above the roaring of the battle, there was a greater roar. The pulpit shuddered and rocked, O'Kelly peeped over the edge. The whole north-western segment of the stadium was a reeking gap through which were pouring McCorkites and O'Kellians. Within seconds there was another roar, and O'Kelly saw the north-eastern segment rise in the air, showering timber and men and bits of men, burst in the air in a black cloud, and subside. Through the gap came new torrents of strugglers. O'Kelly looked with horror out on to the plain, which had the appearance of a furiously blazing forest.

The Prestonians, who were still mainly in the south, soon had the southern half of the stadium level with the north. Now all the several millions on the plain crushed to the centre where O'Kelly stared over the pulpit rim, under the calm flame of the angel.

As far as he could see there were heaving men fighting towards him. It was like a stormy sea viewed from a submarine conning-tower. At any moment it would be over his head.

Directly under him, the O'Kellian main guard was being

hacked to pieces by the superior arms of the Prestonians and the McCorkites, who were thrusting in towards the pulpit from every direction. The slaughter was fearful. Bombs blasted horrible gaps, which closed instantly. Limbs, heads, torn stripped bodies, were tossing on top of the locked, raving mass.

At the bottom of the pulpit, for the first time in his life, O'Kelly prayed.

Then a hand appeared over the pulpit rim. O'Kelly thought for one second that he would throw it off, but instead he crouched down, watching, paralysed. A gasping bloodied blond head appeared.

It was Preston.

He stood upright on the narrow edge of the pulpit. Hands were dragging at him. A swung cutlass hit his knee as he jumped up and caught the bars of the suspended cage.

For a moment he hung there.

Then, with a gasping and wrenching, another head came over the pulpit edge from the opposite side. It was McCaughey. He scrambled up, and, like Preston, jumped. He missed the bars, and hung, with his arms locked around Preston's neck.

O'Kelly saw what would happen.

In a flash, he was out of the pulpit, and with one hazardous leap fell sprawling on to the dense mass of suddenly upstaring faces below. At the same instant the cage came down with a crash, Preston and McCaughey under it.

The pulpit vanished in splinters, the cage wrenched open.

Attackers and defenders fell back.

O'Kelly, on his hands and knees, stared.

'Look! The angel!'

That shout spread across the battlefield like oil across rough water.

From the wreck of the cage the angel was rising. Its head was flung back blazingly erect as ever, its wings folded motionless, flame dripping from its down-pointing toes, as it rose slowly into the air. Its great eyes gazed out beyond the battlefield, beyond the world, beyond the end of space.

It was evening. The sky was a clear darkening blue. The sun had gone down, and the west was dim behind the dark risen atmosphere of battle smoke.

The sound of fighting died away. Soon there was nothing but an unbroken moaning like the lowing of massed cattle, as the wounded bit the grass, and hid their eyes under their upper arms.

The angel rose.

'Look!'

There was a single shout, that seemed to carry over the whole plain. Everyone saw.

Far above the rising angel, in the very apex of the blue heaven, hung a small blazing ring, half the diameter of the moon, in a cloud of yellow radiance.

Slowly it grew larger; it came nearer the earth.

It was a ring of angels.

And, slowly, as they descended, O'Kelly's freed angel rose to meet them.

There were no photographs of this. Every eye on that plain stared and forgot itself.

Two hundred feet up, the angels met, and hung, still. The low continuous moaning of the wounded was like an utter silence.

Then, as slowly, the angels rose together.

All those thousands of bloody eyes stared up.

O'Kelly was upright on his knees, his hands hanging, his head back.

The angels rose.

Smaller, and smaller, grew the bright ring. At last it was only a star. For five long minutes it was a star.

Then the star went out.

Life came back to the plain terribly.

The wounded and the dead lay like the furrows of ploughland. The living stood, and looked at their arms, bloody to the armpits. Then they looked out across the reeking stilled plain. Then they looked at the cage, Preston and McCaughey twisted together under its twisted bars. Then they looked at the blue apex of heaven, which was darker now, and where the ordinary stars were beginning.

Then, finally, they looked at each other.

Snow

And let me repeat this over and over again: beneath my feet is
the earth, some part of the surface of the earth. Beneath the
snow, beneath my feet, that is. What else could it be? It is firm,
I presume, and level. If it is not actually soil and rock, it must
be ice. It is very probably ice. Whichever it may be, it is proof –
the most substantial proof possible – that I am somewhere on
the earth, the known earth. It would be absurd to dig down
through the snow, just to determine exactly what is under-
neath, earth or ice. This bedded snow may well be dozens of
feet deep. Besides, the snow filling all the air and rivering
along the ground would pour into the hole as fast as I could
dig, and cover me too – very quickly.

This could be no other planet: the air is perfectly natural,
perfectly good.

Our aircraft was forced down by this unusual storm. The pilot
tried to make a landing, but misjudged the extraordinary power
of the wind and the whereabouts of the ground. The crash was
violent. The fuselage buckled and gaped, and I was flung clear.
Unconscious of everything save the need to get away from the
disaster, I walked farther off into the blizzard and collapsed,
which explains why when I came to full consciousness and
stood up out of the snow that was burying me I could see
nothing of either the aircraft or my fellow passengers. All

around me was what I have been looking at ever since. The bottomless dense motion of snow. I started to walk.

Of course, everything previous to that first waking may have been entirely different since I don't remember a thing about it. Whatever chance dropped me here in the snow evidently destroyed my memory. That's one thing of which there is no doubt whatsoever. It is, so to speak, one of my facts. The aircraft crash is a working hypothesis, that merely.

There's no reason why I should not last quite a long time yet. I seem to have an uncommon reserve of energy. To keep my mind firm, that is the essential thing, to fix it firmly in my reasonable hopes, and lull it there, encourage it. Mesmerize it slightly with a sort of continuous prayer. Because when my mind is firm, my energy is firm. And that's the main thing here – energy. No matter how circumspect I may be, or how lucid, without energy I am lost on the spot. Useless to think about it. Where my energy ends I end, and all circumspection and all lucidity with me. As long as I have energy I can correct my mistakes, outlast them, outwalk them – for instance the unimaginable error that as far as I know I am making at this very moment. This step, this, the next five hundred, or five thousand – all mistaken, all absolute waste, back to where I was ten hours ago. But we recognize that thought. My mind is not my friend. My support, my defence, but my enemy too – not perfectly intent on getting me out of this. If I were mindless perhaps there would be no difficulty whatsoever. I would simply go on, aware of nothing but my step by step success in getting over the ground. The thing to do is to keep alert, keep my mind fixed in alertness, recognize these treacherous paralysing, yes, lethal thoughts the second they enter, catch them before they can make that burrowing plunge down the spinal cord.

Then gently and without any other acknowledgement push

them back – out into the snow where they belong. And that *is* where they belong. They are infiltrations of the snow, encroachments of this immensity of lifelessness. But they enter so slyly! We are true, they say or at least very probably true, and on that account you must entertain us and even give us the run of your life, since above all things you are dedicated to the truth. That is the air they have, that's how they come in. What do I know about the truth? As if simple-minded dedication to truth were the final law of existence! I only know more and more clearly what is good for me. It's my mind that has this contemptible awe for the probably true, and my mind, I know, I prove it every minute, is not me and is by no means sworn to help me. Am I to lie? I must survive – that's a truth sacred as any, and as the hungry truths devour the sleepy truths I shall digest every other possible truth to the substance and health and energy of my own, and the ones I can't digest I shall spit out, since in this situation my intention to survive is the one mouth, the one digestive tract, so to speak, by which I live. But those others! I relax for a moment, I leave my mind to itself for a moment – and they are in complete possession. They plunge into me, exultantly, mercilessly. There is no question of their intention or their power. Five seconds of carelessness, and they have struck. The strength melts from me, my bowels turn to water, my consciousness darkens and shrinks, I have to stop.

What are my facts? I do have some definite facts.

Taking six steps every five seconds, I calculate – allowing for my brief regular sleeps – that I have been walking through this blizzard for five months and during that time have covered something equal to the breadth of the Atlantic between Southampton and New York. Two facts. And a third: throughout those five months this twilight of snow has not grown either darker or brighter.

So.

There seems no reason to doubt that I am somewhere within either the Arctic or the Antarctic Circle. That's a comfort, it means my chances of survival are not uniquely bad. Men have walked the length of Asia simply to amuse themselves.

Obviously I am not travelling in a straight line. But that needn't give me any anxiety. Perhaps I made a mistake when I first started walking, setting my face against the wind instead of downwind. Coming against the wind I waste precious energy and there is always this wearisome snow blocking my eyes and mouth. But I had to trust the wind. This resignation to the wind's guidance is the foundation of my firmness of mind. The wind is not simply my compass. In fact, I must not think of it as a compass at all. The wind is my law. As a compass nothing could be more useless. No need to dwell on that. It's extremely probable, indeed, and something I need not hide from myself, that this wind is leading me to and fro in quite a tight little maze – always shifting too stealthily for me to notice the change. Or, if the sun is circling the horizon, it seems likely that the wind is swinging with it through the 360 degrees once in every twenty-four hours, turning me as I keep my face against it in a perfect circle not more than seven miles across. This would explain the otherwise strange fact that in spite of the vast distance I have covered the terrain is still dead level, exactly as when I started. A frozen lake, no doubt. This is a strong possibility and I must get used to it without letting it overwhelm me, and without losing sight of its real advantages.

The temptation to trust to luck and instinct and cut out across the wind is to be restricted. The effect on my system of confidence would be disastrous. My own judgement would naturally lead me in a circle. I would have to make deliberate changes of direction to break out of that circle – only to go in a larger circle or a circle in the opposite direction. So more changes. Wilder and more sudden changes, changes of my changes – all to evade an enemy that showed so little sign of itself it might as well not have existed. It's clear where all that would end. Shouting and running and so on. Staggering round like a man beset by a mob. Falling, grovelling. So on. The snow.

No. All I have to do is endure: that is, keep my face to the wind. My face to the wind, a firm grip on my mind, and everything else follows naturally. There is not the slightest need to be anxious. Any time now the polar night will arrive, bringing a drastic change of climate – inevitable. Clearing the sky and revealing the faultless compass of the stars.

The facts are overwhelmingly on my side. I could almost believe in Providence. After all, if one single circumstance were slightly – only slightly – other than it is! If, for instance, instead of waking in a blizzard on a firm level place I had come to consciousness falling endlessly through snow-cloud. Then I might have wondered very seriously whether I were in the gulf or not. Or if the atmosphere happened to consist of, say, ammonia. I could not have survived more than a moment. And in that moment before death by asphyxiation I would certainly have been convinced I was out on some lifeless planet. Or if I had no body but simply arms and legs growing out of a head, my whole system of confidence would have been disoriented from the start. My dreams, for instance, would have been meaningless to me, or rather an argument of my own meaninglessness. I would have died almost immediately, out of sheer bewilderment. It wouldn't need nearly such extreme differences either. If I had been without these excellent pigskin boots, trousers, jacket, gloves and hood, the cold would have extinguished me at once.

And even if I had double the clothing that I have, where would I be without my chair? My chair is quite as important as one of my lungs. As both my lungs, indeed, for without it I would be dead. Where would I have slept? Lying in the snow. But lying flat, as I have discovered, I am buried by the snow in just under a minute, and the cold begins to take over my hands and my feet and my face. Sleep would be impossible. In other words, I would very soon collapse of exhaustion and be buried. As it is, I unsnap my chair harness, plant the chair in the snow, sit on it, set my feet on the rung between the front legs, my arms folded over my knees and my head resting on my arms, and am able in this way to take a sleep of fully ten minutes before the snow piles over me.

The chain of providential coincidences is endless. Or rather, like a chain-mail, it is complete without one missing link to betray and annul the rest. Even my dreams are part of it. They are as tough and essential a link as any, since there can no longer be any doubt that they are an accurate reproduction of my whole previous life, of the world as it is and as I knew it – all without one contradictory detail. Yet if my amnesia had been only a little bit stronger! – it needed only that. Because without this evidence of the world and my identity I could have known no purpose in continuing the ordeal. I could only have looked, breathed and died, like a nestling fallen from the nest.

Everything fits together. And the result – my survival, and my determination to survive. I should rejoice.

The chair is of conventional type: nothing in the least mystifying about it. A farmhouse sort of chair: perfectly of a piece with my dreams, as indeed are my clothes, my body and all the inclinations of my mind. It is of wood, painted black, though in places showing a coat of brown beneath the black. One of the nine struts in the back is missing and some child – I suppose it was a child – has stuck a dab of chewing-gum into the empty socket. Obviously the chair has been well used, and not too carefully. The right foreleg has been badly chewed, evidently by a puppy, and on the seat both black and brown paints are wearing through showing the dark grain of the pale wood. If all this is not final evidence of a reality beyond my own, of the reality of the world it comes from, the world I re-dream in my sleeps – I might as well lie down in the snow and be done with.

The curious harness needn't worry me. The world, so far as I've dreamed it at this point, contains no such harness, true. But since I've not yet dreamed anything from after my twenty-sixth birthday, the harness might well have been invented between that time and the time of my disaster. Probably it's now in general use. Or it may be the paraphernalia of some fashionable game that came in during my twenty-seventh or later year, and to which I got addicted. Sitting on snow peaks in nineteenth-century chairs. Or perhaps I developed a passion for painting polar scenery and along with that a passion for this particular chair as my painting seat, and had the harness designed specially. A lucky eccentricity! It is perfectly adapted to my present need. But all that's in the dark still. There's a lot I haven't dreamed yet. From my twenty-third and twenty-fourth years I have almost nothing – a few insignificant episodes. Nothing at all after my twenty-sixth birthday. The rest, though, is about complete, which suggests that any time now I ought to be getting my twenty-third and twenty-fourth years in full and, more important, my twenty-seventh year, or as much of it as there is, along with the accurate account of my disaster and the origin of my chair.

There seems little doubt of my age. Had I been dreaming my life chronologically there would have been real cause for worry. I could have had no idea how much was still to come. Of course, if I were suddenly to dream something from the middle of my sixtieth year I would have to reorganize all my ideas. What really convinces me of my youth is my energy. The appearance of my body tells me nothing. Indeed, from my hands and feet – which are all I have dared to uncover – one could believe I was several hundred years old, or even dead, they are so black and shrunken on the bone. But the emaciation is understandable, considering that for five months I have been living exclusively on will-power, without the slightest desire for food.

I have my job to get back to, and my mother and father will be in despair. And God knows what will have happened to Helen. Did I marry her? I have no wedding ring. But we were engaged. And it is another confirmation of my youth that my feelings for her are as they were then – stronger, in fact, yes, a good deal stronger, though speaking impartially these feelings that seem to be for her might easily be nothing but my desperate longing to get back to the world in general – a longing that is using my one-time affection for Helen as a sort of form or model. It's possible, very possible, that I have in reality forgotten her, even that I am sixty years old, that she has been dead for thirty-four years. Certain things may be very different from what I imagine. If I were to take this drift of thoughts to the logical extreme there is no absolute proof that my job, my parents, Helen and the whole world are not simply my own invention, fantasies my imagination has improvised on the simple themes of my own form, my clothes, my chair, and the properties of my present environment. I am in no position to be sure about anything.

But there is more to existence, fortunately, than consideration of possibilities. There is conviction, faith. If there were not, where would I be? The moment I allow one of these 'possibilities' the slightest intimacy – a huge futility grips me, as it were physically, by the heart, as if the organ itself were despairing of this life and ready to give up.

Snow

Courageous and calm. That should be my prayer. I should repeat that, repeat it like the Buddhists with their 'O jewel of the lotus'. Repeat it till it repeats itself in my very heart, till every heartbeat drives it through my whole body. Courageous and calm. This is the world, think no more about it.

My chair will keep me sane. My chair, my chair, my chair – I might almost repeat that. I know every mark on it, every grain. So near and true! It alone predicates a universe, the entire universe, with its tough carpentry, its sprightly, shapely design – so delicate, so strong. And while I have the game I need be afraid of nothing. Though it is dangerous. Tempting, dangerous, but – it is enough to know that the joy is mine. I set the chair down in the snow, letting myself think I am going to sleep, but instead of sitting I step back a few paces into the snow. How did I think of that? The first time, I did not dare look away from it. I had never before let it out of my hand, never let it go for a fraction between unbuckling it and sitting down on it. But then I let it go and stepped back into the snow. I had never heard my voice before. I was astonished at the sound that struggled up out of me. Well, I need the compensations. And this game does rouse my energies, so it is, in a sense, quite practical. After the game, I could run. That's the moment of danger, though, the moment of overpowering impatience when I could easily lose control and break out, follow my instinct, throw myself on luck, run out across the wind.

But there is a worse danger. If I ran out across the wind I would pretty soon come to my senses, turn my face back into the wind. It is the game itself, the stage of development it has reached, that is dangerous now. I no longer simply step back. I set the chair down, turn my face away and walk off into the blizzard, counting my steps carefully. At fourteen paces I stop. Fifteen is the limit of vision in this dense flow of snow, so at fourteen I stop, and turn. Let those be the rules. Let me fix the game at that. Because at first I see nothing. That should be enough for me. Everywhere, pouring silent grey, a silence like a pressure, like the slow coming to bear of some incalculable pressure, too gradual to detect. If I were simply to stand there my mind would crack in a few moments. But I concentrate, I withdraw my awe from the emptiness and look pointedly into it. At first, everything is as usual – as I have seen it for five months. Then my heart begins to thump unnaturally, because I seem to make out a dimness, a shadow that wavers deep in the grey turmoil, vanishes and darkens, rises and falls. I step one pace forward and using all my will-power stop again. The shadow is as it was. Another step. The shadow seems to be a little darker. Then it vanishes and I lunge two steps forward but immediately stop because there it is, quite definite, no longer moving. Slowly I walk towards it. The rules are that I keep myself under control, and I restrain all sobs or shouts, though of course it is impossible to keep the breathing regular – at this stage at least, and right up to the point where the shadow resolves into a chair. In that vast grey dissolution – my chair! The snowflakes are drifting against the legs and gliding between the struts, bumping against them, clinging and crawling over the seat. To control myself then is not within human power. Indeed I seem to more or less lose consciousness at that point. I'm certainly not responsible for the weeping, shouting thing that falls on my chair, embracing it, kissing it, bruising his cheeks against it. As the snowflakes tap and run over my gloves and over the chair I begin to call them names. I peer into each one as if it were a living face, full of speechless recognition, and I call to them – Willy, Joanna, Peter, Jesus, Ferdinand, anything that comes into my head, and shout to them and nod and laugh. Well, it's a harmless enough madness.

The temptation to go beyond the fourteen paces is now becoming painful. To go deep into the blizzard. Forty paces. Then come back, peering. Fifteen paces, twenty paces. Stop. A shadow.

That would not be harmless madness. If I were to leave my chair like that the chances are I would never find it again. My footprints do not exist in this undertow of snow. Weeks later, I would still be searching, casting in great circles, straining at every moment to pry a shadow out of the grey sameness. My chair meanwhile a hundred miles away in the blizzard, motionless – neat legs and elegant back, sometimes buried, sometimes uncovering again. And for centuries, long after I'm finished, still sitting there, intact with its tooth-marks and missing strut, waiting for a darkening shape to come up out of the nothingness and shout to it and fall on it and possess it.

But my chair is here, on my back, here. There's no danger of my ever losing it. Never so long as I keep control, keep my mind firm. All the facts are on my side. I have nothing to do but endure.

Sunday

Michael marched off to chapel beside his sister, rapping his Sunday shoes down on to the pavement to fetch the brisk, stinging echo off housewalls, wearing the detestable blue blazer with its meaningless badge as a uniform loaded with honours and privilege. In chapel he sat erect, arms folded, instead of curling down on to his spine like a prawn and sinking his chin between his collar-bones as under the steady pressure of a great hand, which was his usual attitude of worship. He sang the hymns and during the prayers thought exultantly of Top Wharf Pub, trying to remember what time those places opened.

All this zest, however, was no match for the sermon. The minister's voice soared among the beams, tireless, as if he were still rehearsing, and after ten minutes these organ-like modulations began to work Michael into a torment of impatience. The nerve-ends all over his body prickled and swarmed. He almost had to sink to his knees. Thoughts of shouting, 'Oh, well!' – one enormous sigh, or simply running out of chapel, brought a fine sweat on to his temples. Finally he closed his eyes and began to imagine a wolf galloping through snow-filled, moonlit forest. Without fail this image was the first thing in his mind whenever he shut his eyes on these situations of constraint, in school, in waiting-rooms, with visitors. The wolf urged itself with all its strength through a land empty of everything but trees and snow. After a while he drifted to vaguer things, a few moments of freedom before his impatience jerked him back to see how the sermon was doing. It was still soaring. He closed his eyes and the wolf was there again.

By the time the doors opened, letting light stream in, he felt stupefied. He edged out with the crowd. Then the eleven-o'clock Sunday sky struck him. He had forgotten it was so early in the day. But with the light and the outside world his mind returned in a rush. Leaving his sister deep in the chapel, buried in a pink and blue bouquet of her friends, and evading the minister who, having processed his congregation generally within, had darted round the side of the chapel to the porch and was now setting his personal seal, a crushing smile and a soft, supporting handclasp, on each member of the flock as they stumbled out, Michael took the three broad steps at a leap and dodged down the crowded path among the graves, like a person with an important dispatch.

But he was no sooner out through the gate than the stitches of his shoes seemed suddenly to tighten, and his damped hair tightened on his scalp. He slowed to a walk,

To the farthest skyline it was Sunday. The valley walls, throughout the week wet, hanging, uncomfortable woods and mud-hole farms, were today neat, remote, and irreproachably pretty, postcard pretty. The blue sky, the sparklingly smoke-less Sunday air, had disinfected them. Picnickers and chapel-hikers were already up there, sprinkled like confetti along the steep lanes and paths, creeping imperceptibly upward towards the brown line of the moors. Spotless, harmless, church-going slopes! Life, over the whole countryside, was suspended for the day.

Below him the town glittered in the clear air and sunlight.

Throughout the week it resembled from this point a volcanic pit, bottomless in places, a jagged fissure into a sulphurous underworld, the smoke dragging off the chimneys of the mills and house-rows like a tearing fleece. Now it lay as under shallow, slightly warm, clear water, with still streets and bright yards.

There was even something Sundayish about the pavements, something untouchably proper, though nothing had gone over them since grubby Saturday except more feet and darkness.

Superior to all this for once, and quite enjoying it again now he was on his way, Michael went down the hill into the town with strides that jammed his toes into the ends of his shoes. He turned into the Memorial Gardens, past prams, rockeries, forbidden grass, trees with labels, and over the ornamental canal bridge to the bowling greens that lay on the level between canal and river.

His father was there, on the farthest green, with two familiar figures – Harry Rutley, the pork butcher, and Mr Stinson, a tall, sooty, lean man who held his head as if he were blind and spoke rarely, and then only as if phrasing his most private thoughts to himself. A man Michael preferred not to look at. Michael sat on a park bench behind their jack and tried to make himself obvious.

The paths were full of people. Last night this had been a parade of couples, foursomes, gangs and lonely ones – the electricity gathered off looms, sewing-machines and shop counters since Monday milling round the circuit and discharging up the sidepaths among the shrubbery in giggling darkness and shrieks. But now it was families, an after-chapel procession of rustlings and murmurings, lacy bosoms, tight blue pinstripe suits and daisy-chains of children. Soon Michael was worn out, willing the bowls against their bias or against the crown of the green or to roll one foot farther and into the trough or to collide and fall in halves. He could see the Wesleyan Church clock at quarter past eleven and stared at it for what seemed like five minutes, convinced it had stopped.

He stood up as the three men came over to study the pattern of the bowls.

'Are we going now, Dad?'

'Just a minute, lad. Come and have a game.'

That meant at least another game whether he played or not. Another quarter of an hour! And to go and get out a pair of bowls was as good as agreeing to stay there playing till one.

'We might miss him.'

His father laughed. Only just remembering his promise, thought Michael.

'He'll not be there till well on. We shan't miss him.'

His father kicked his bowls together and Harry Rutley slewed the rubber mat into position.

'But will he be there sure?'

Sunday dinner was closer every minute. Then it was sleepy Sunday afternoon. Then Aunt-infested Sunday tea. His father laughed again.

'Billy Red'll be coming down today, won't he, Harry?'

Harry Rutley, pale, slow, round, weighed his jack. He had lost the tip of an ear at the Dardanelles and carried a fragment of his fifth rib on the end of his watch-chain. Now he narrowed his eyes, choosing a particular blade of grass on the far corner of the green.

'Bill Red? Every Sunday. Twelve on the dot.' He dipped his body to the underswing of his arm and came upright as the jack curled away across the green. 'I don't know how he does it.'

The jack had come to rest two feet from the far corner. There followed four more games. They played back to Michael, then across to the far right, then a short one down to the far left, then back to the near right. At last the green was too full, with nine or ten games interweaving and shouts of 'feet' every other minute and bowls bocking together in mid-green.

At quarter to twelve on the clock – Michael now sullen with the punishment he had undergone and the certainty that his day had been played away – the three men came off the green, put away their bowls, and turned down on to the canal bank tow-path.

The valley became narrower and its sides steeper. Road, river and canal made their way as best they could, with only a twenty-yard strip of wasteland – a tangle of rank weeds, elderberry bushes and rubble, bleached debris of floods – separating river and canal. Along the far side of the river squeezed the road, rumbling from Monday to Saturday with swaying lorry-loads of cotton and wool and cloth. The valley wall on that side, draped with a network of stone-walled fields and precariously clinging farms and woods, came down sheer out of the sky into the backyards of a crouched stone row of weavers' cottages whose front doorsteps were almost part of the road. The river ran noisily over pebbles. On the strip of land between river and canal stood Top Wharf pub – its buildings tucked in under the bank of the canal so that the tow-path ran level with the back bedroom window. On this side the valley wall, with overshadowing woods, dived straight into the black, motionless canal as if it must be a mile deep. The water was quite shallow, however, with its collapsed banks and accumulation of mud, so shallow that in some places the rushes grew right across. For years it had brought nothing to Top Wharf Pub but a black greasy damp and rats.

They turned down off the tow-path into the wide, cobbled yard in front of the pub.

'You sit here. Now what would you like to drink?'

Michael sat on the cracked, weather-scrubbed bench in the yard under the bar-room window and asked for ginger beer.

'And see if he's come yet. And see if they have any rats ready.'

He had begun to notice the heat and now leaned back against the wall to get the last slice of shade under the eaves. But in no time the sun had moved out over the yard. The valley sides funnelled its rays down as into a trap, dazzling the quartz-points of the worn cobbles, burning the colour off everything. The flies were going wild, swirling in the air, darting and basking on the cobbles – big, green-glossed bluebottles that leapt on to his hand when he laid it along the hot bench.

In twos and threes men came over the hog-backed bridge leading from the road into the yard, or down off the tow-path. Correct, leisurely and a little dazed from morning service, or in overalls that were torn and whitened from obscure Sabbath labours, all disappeared through the door. The hubbub inside thickened. Michael strained to catch some mention of Billy Red.

At last his father brought him his ginger beer and informed him that Billy Red had not arrived yet but everybody was expecting him and he shouldn't be long. They had some nice rats ready.

In spite of the heat, Michael suddenly did not feel like drinking. His whole body seemed to have become frailer and slightly faint, as with hunger. When he sipped, the liquid trickled with a cold, tasteless weight into his disinterested stomach.

He left the glass on the bench and went to the Gents. Afterwards he walked stealthily round the yard, looking in at the old stables and coach-house, the stony cave silences. Dust, cobwebs, rat droppings. Old timbers, old wheels, old harness.

Barrels, and rusty stoves. He listened for rats. Walking back across the blinding, humming yard he smelt roast beef and heard the clattering of the pub kitchen and saw through the open window fat arms working over a stove. The whole world was at routine Sunday dinner. The potatoes were already steaming, people sitting about killing time and getting impatient and wishing that something would fall out of the blue and knowing that nothing would. The idea stifled him, he didn't want to think of it. He went quickly back to the bench and sat down, his heart beating as if he had run.

A car nosed over the little bridge and stopped at the far side of the yard, evidently not sure whether it was permitted to enter the yard at all. Out of it stepped a well-to-do young man and a young woman. The young man unbuttoned his pale tweed jacket, thrust his hands into his trouser pockets and came sauntering towards the pub door, the girl on her high heels following beside him, patting her hair and looking round at the scenery as if she had just come up out of a dark pit. They stood at the door for a moment, improvising their final decisions about what she would drink, whether this was the right place, and whether she ought to come in. He was sure it was the right place, this was where they did it all right, and he motioned to her to sit on the end of the bench beside Michael. Michael moved accommodatingly to the other end. She ignored him, however, and perched on the last ten inches of the bench, arrayed her wide-skirted, summery, blue-flowered frock over her knees, and busied herself with her mirror. The flies whirled around, inspecting this new thing of scents.

Suddenly there came a shout from the doorway of the pub, long-drawn words: 'Here comes the man.'

Immediately several crowded to the doorway, glasses in their hands.

'Here he comes.'

'The Red Killer!'

'Poor little beggar. He looks as if he lives on rat meat.'

'Draw him a half, Gab.'

Over the bridge and into the yard shambled a five-foot ragged figure. Scarecrowish, tawny to colourless, exhausted, this was Billy Red, the rat-catcher. As a sideline he kept hens, and he had something of the raw, flea-bitten look of a red hen, with his small, sunken features and gingery hair. From the look of his clothes you would think he slept on the hen-house floor, under the roosts. One hand in his pocket, his back at a half-bend, he drifted aimlessly to a stop. Then, to show that after all he had only come for a sit in the sun, he sat down beside Michael with a long sigh.

'It's a grand day,' he announced. His voice was not strong – lungless, a shaky wisp, full of hen-fluff and dust.

Michael peered closely and secretly at this wrinkled neglected fifty-year-old face shrunk on its small skull. Among the four-day stubble and enlarged pores and deep folds it was hard to make out anything, but there were one or two marks that might have been old rat bites. He had a little withered mouth and kept moving the lips about as if he couldn't get them comfortable. After a sigh he would pause a minute, leaning forward, one elbow on his knees, then sigh again, changing his position, the other elbow now on the other knee, like a man too weary to rest.

'Here you are, Billy.'

A hand held a half-pint high at the pub door like a sign and with startling readiness Billy leapt to his feet and disappeared into the pub, gathering the half-pint on the way and saying:

'I've done a daft bloody thing. I've come down all this way wi'out brass.'

There was an obliging roar of laughter and Michael found himself looking at the girl's powdered profile. She was staring down at her neatly covered toe as it twisted this way and that, presenting all its polished surfaces.

Things began to sound livelier inside – sharp, loud remarks kicking up bursts of laughter and showering exclamations. The young man came out, composed, serious, and handed the girl a long-stemmed clear glass with a cherry in it. He sat down between her and Michael, splaying his knees as he did so and lunging his face forward to meet his streamingly raised pint – one smooth, expert motion.

'He's in there now,' he said, wiping his mouth. 'They're getting him ready.'

The girl gazed into his face, tilting her glass till the cherry bobbed against her pursed red lips, opening her eyes wide.

Michael looked past her to the doorway. A new figure had appeared. He supposed this must be the landlord, Gab – an aproned hemisphere and round, red greasy face that screwed itself up to survey the opposite hillside.

'Right,' called the landlord. 'I'll get 'em.' Away he went, wiping his hands on his apron, then letting them swing wide of his girth like penguin flippers, towards the coach-house. Now everybody came out of the pub and Michael stood up, surprised to see how many had been crowded in there. They were shouting and laughing, pausing to browse their pints, circulating into scattered groups. Michael went over and stood beside his father, who was one of an agitated four. He had to ask twice before he could make himself heard. Even to himself his voice sounded thinner than usual, empty, as if at bottom it wanted nothing so much as to dive into his stomach and hide there in absolute silence, letting events go their own way.

'How many is he going to do?'

'I think they've got two.' His father half turned down towards him. 'It's usually two or three.'

Nobody took any notice of Billy Red, who was standing a

little apart, his hands hanging down from the slight stoop that seemed more or less permanent with him, smiling absently at the noisy, hearty groups. He brightened and straightened as the last man out of the pub came across, balancing a brimming pint glass. Michael watched. The moment the pint touched those shrivelled lips the pale little eye set with a sudden strangled intentness. His long, skinny, unshaven throat writhed and the beer shrank away in the glass. In two or three seconds he lowered the glass empty, wiped his mouth on his sleeve and looked around. Then, as nobody stepped forward to offer him a fill-up, he set the glass down to the cobbles and stood drying his hands on his jacket.

Michael's gaze shifted slightly, and he saw the girl. He recognized his own thoughts in her look of mesmerized incredulity. At her side the young man was watching too, but shrewdly, between steady drinks.

The sun seemed to have come to a stop directly above. Two or three men had taken their jackets off, with irrelevant, noisy clowning, a few sparring feints. Somebody suggested they all go and stand in the canal and Billy Red do his piece under water, and another laughed so hard at this that the beer came spurting from his nostrils. High up on the opposite slope Michael could see a line of Sunday walkers, moving slowly across the dazed grey of the fields. Their coats would be over their shoulders, their ties in their pockets, their shoes agony, the girls asking to be pushed – but if they stood quite still they would feel a breeze. In the cobbled yard the heat had begun to dance.

'Here we are.'

The landlord waddled into the middle of the yard holding up an oblong wire cage. He set it down with a clash on the cobbles.

'Two of the best.'

Everybody crowded round. Michael squeezed to the front and crouched down beside the cage. There was a pause of admiration. Hunched in opposite corners of the cage, their heads low and drawn in and their backs pressed to the wires so that the glossy black-tipped hairs bristled out, were two big brown rats. They sat quiet. A long pinkish-grey tail, thick at the root as his thumb, coiled out by Michael's foot. He touched the hairy tip of it gently with his forefinger.

'Watch out, lad!'

The rat snatched its tail in, leapt across the cage with a crash and, gripping one of the zinc bars behind its curved yellow teeth, shook till the cage rattled. The other rat left its corner and began gliding to and fro along one side – a continuous low fluidity, sniffing up and down the bars. Then both rats stopped and sat up on their hind legs, like persons coming out of a trance, suddenly recognizing people. Their noses quivered as they directed their set, grey-chinned, inquisitive expressions at one face after another.

The landlord had been loosening the nooses in the end of two long pieces of dirty string. He lifted the cage again.

'Catch a tail, Walt.'

The group pressed closer. A hand came out and roamed in readiness under the high-held cage floor. The rats moved uneasily. The landlord gave the cage a shake and the rats crashed. A long tail swung down between the wires. The hand grabbed and pulled.

'Hold it.'

The landlord slipped the noose over the tail, down to the very butt, and pulled it tight. The caught rat, not quite convinced before but now understanding the whole situation, doubled round like a thing without bones, and bit and shook the bars and forced its nose out between them to get at the string that held its buttocks tight to the cage side.

'Just hold that string, Walt. So's it can't get away when we open up.'

Now the landlord lifted the cage again, while Walt held his string tight. The other rat, watching the operation on its companion, had bunched up in a corner, sitting on its tail.

'Clever little beggar. You know what I'm after, don't you?'

The landlord gave the cage a shake, but the rat clung on, its pink feet gripping the wires of the cage floor like hands. He shook the cage violently.

'Move, you stubborn little beggar,' demanded the landlord. He went on shaking the cage with sharp, jerking movements.

Then the rat startled everybody. Squeezing still farther into its corner, it opened its mouth wide and began to scream – a harsh, ripping, wavering scream travelling out over the yard like some thin, metallic, dazzling substance that decomposed instantly. As one scream died the rat started another, its mouth wide. Michael had never thought a rat could make so much noise. As it went on at full intensity, his stomach began to twist and flex like a thick muscle. For a moment he was so worried by these sensations that he stopped looking at the rat. The landlord kept on shaking the cage and the scream shook in the air, but the rat clung on, still sitting on its tail.

'Give him a poke, Gab, stubborn little beggar!'

The landlord held the cage still, reached into his top pocket and produced a pencil. At this moment, Michael saw the girl, extricating herself from the press, pushing out backwards. The ring of rapt faces and still legs closed again. The rat was hurtling round the cage, still screaming, leaping over the other, attacking the wires first at this side then at that. All at once it crouched in a corner, silent. A hand came out and grabbed the loop of tail. The other noose was there ready. The landlord set the cage down.

Now the circle relaxed and everyone looked down at the two

rats flattened on the cage bottom, their tails waving foolishly outside the wires.

'Well then, Billy,' said the landlord. 'How are they?'

Billy Red nodded and grinned.

'Them's grand,' he said. 'Grand.' His little rustling voice made Michael want to cough.

'Right. Stand back.'

Everybody backed obediently, leaving the cage, Walt with his foot on one taut string and the landlord with his foot on the other in the middle of an arena six or seven yards across. Michael saw the young man on the far side, his glass still half full in his hand. The girl was nowhere to be seen.

Billy Red peeled off his coat, exposing an old shirt, army issue, most of the left arm missing. He pulled his trousers up under his belt, spat on his hands, and took up a position which placed the cage door a couple of paces or so from his left side and slightly in front of him. He bent forward a little more than usual, his arms hanging like a wary wrestler's, his eye fixed on the cage.

'Eye like a bloody sparrow-hawk,' somebody murmured.

There was silence. The landlord waited, kneeling now beside the cage. Nothing disturbed the dramatic moment but the distant, brainless church bells.

'This one first, Walt,' said the landlord. 'Ready, Billy?'

He pushed down the lever that raised the cage door and let his rat have its full five- or six-yard length of string. He had the end looped around his hand. Walt kept his rat on a tight string.

Everybody watched intently. The freed rat pulled its tail in delicately and sniffed at the noose round it, ignoring the wide-open door. Then the landlord reached to tap the cage and in a flash the rat vanished.

Michael lost sight of it. But he saw Billy Red spin half round and drop smack down on his hands and knees on the cobbles.

'He's got it!'

Billy Red's face was compressed in a snarl and as he snapped his head from side to side the dark, elongated body of the rat whipped around his neck. He had it by the shoulders. Michael's eyes fixed like cameras.

A dozen shakes, and Billy Red stopped, his head lowered. The rat hanging from his mouth was bunching and relaxing, bunching and relaxing. He waited. Everyone waited. Then the rat spasmed, fighting with all its paws, and Billy shook again wildly, the rat's tail flying like a lash. This time when he stopped the body hung down limply. The piece of string, still attached to the tail, trailed away across the cobbles.

Gently Billy took the rat from his mouth and laid it down. He stood up, spat a couple of times, and began to wipe his mouth, smiling shamefacedly. Everybody breathed out – an exclamation of marvelling disgust and admiration, and loud above the rest:

'Pint now, Billy?'

The landlord walked back into the pub and most of the audience followed him to refresh their glasses. Billy Red stood separate, still wiping his mouth with a scrap of snuff-coloured cloth.

Michael went over and bent to look at the dead rat. Its shoulders were wet-black with saliva, and the fur bitten. It lay on its left side, slightly curved, its feet folded, its eyes still round and bright in their alert, inquisitive expression. He touched its long, springy whiskers. A little drip of blood was puddling under its nose on the cobblestones. As he watched, a bluebottle alighted on its tail and sprang off again, then suddenly reappeared on its nose, inspecting the blood.

He walked over to the cage. Walt was standing there talking, his foot on the taut string. This rat crouched against the wires as if they afforded some protection. It made no sign of noticing

Michael as he bent low over it. Its black beads stared outward fixedly, its hot brown flanks going in and out. There was a sparkle on its fur, and as he looked more closely, thinking it must be perspiration, he became aware of the heat again.

He stood up, a dull pain in his head. He put his hand to his scalp and pressed the scorch down into his skull, but that didn't seem to connect with the dull, thick pain.

'I'm off now, Dad,' he called.

'Already? Aren't you going to see this other one?'

'I think I'll go.' He set off across the yard.

'Finish your drink,' his father called after him.

He saw his glass almost full on the end of the white bench but walked past it and round the end of the pub and up on to the tow-path. The sycamore trees across the canal arched over black damp shade and the still water. High up, the valley slopes were silvered now, frizzled with the noon brightness. The earthen tow-path was like stone. Fifty yards along he passed the girl in the blue-flowered frock sauntering back towards the pub, pulling at the heads of the tall bank grasses.

'Have they finished yet?' she asked.

Michael shook his head. He found himself unable to speak. With all his strength he began to run.

The Rain Horse

As the young man came over the hill the first thin blowing of rain met him. He turned his coat-collar up and stood on top of the shelving rabbit-riddled hedge bank, looking down into the valley.

He had come too far. What had set out as a walk along pleasantly remembered tarmac lanes had turned dreamily by gate and path and hedge-gap into a cross-ploughland trek, his shoes ruined, the dark mud of the lower fields inching up the trouser legs of his grey suit where they rubbed against each other. And now there was a raw, flapping wetness in the air that would be downpour again at any minute. He shivered, holding himself tense against the cold.

This was the view he had been thinking of. Vaguely, without really directing his walk, he had felt he would get the whole thing from this point. For twelve years, whenever he had recalled this scene, he had imagined it as it looked from here. Now the valley lay sunken in front of him, utterly deserted, shallow, bare fields, black and sodden as the bed of an ancient lake after the weeks of rain.

Nothing happened. Not that he had looked forward to any very transfiguring experience. But he had expected something, some pleasure, some meaningful sensation, he didn't quite know what.

So he waited, trying to nudge the right feelings alive with the details – the surprisingly familiar curve of the hedges, the stone gate-pillar and iron gatehook let into it that he had used as a target, the long bank of the rabbit-warren on which he stood and which had been the first thing he ever noticed about the hill when, twenty years ago, from the distance of the village, he had said to himself, 'That looks like rabbits.'

Twelve years had changed him. This land no longer recognized him, and he looked back at it coldly, as at a finally visited home-country, known only through the stories of a grandfather; felt nothing but the dullness of feeling nothing. Boredom. Then, suddenly, impatience, with a whole exasperated swarm of little anxieties about his shoes, and the spitting rain and his new suit and that sky and the two-mile trudge through the mud to the road.

It would be quicker to go straight forward to the farm a mile away in the valley and behind which the road looped. But the thought of meeting the farmer – to be embarrassingly remembered or shouted at as a trespasser – deterred him. He saw the rain pulling up out of the distance, dragging its grey broken columns, smudging the trees and the farms.

A wave of anger went over him: anger against himself for blundering into this mud-trap and anger against the land that made him feel so outcast, so old and stiff and stupid. He wanted nothing but to get away from it as quickly as possible. But as he turned, something moved in his eye-corner. All his senses startled alert. He stopped.

Over to his right a thin, black horse was running across the ploughland towards the hill, its head down, neck stretched out. It seemed to be running on its toes like a cat, like a dog up to no good.

From the high point on which he stood the hill dipped slightly and rose to another crested point fringed with the tops of trees, three hundred yards to his right. As he watched it, the horse ran up to that crest, showed against the sky – for a moment like a nightmarish leopard – and disappeared over the other side.

For several seconds he stared at the skyline, stunned by the unpleasantly strange impression the horse had made on him. Then the plastering beat of icy rain on his bare skull brought him to himself. The distance had vanished in a wall of grey. All around him the fields were jumping and streaming.

Holding his collar close and tucking his chin down into it, he ran back over the hilltop towards the town-side, the lee-side, his feet sucking and splashing, at every stride plunging to the ankle.

This hill was shaped like a wave, a gently rounded back lifting out of the valley to a sharply crested, almost concave front hanging over the river meadows towards the town. Down this front, from the crest, hung two small woods separated by a fallow field. The near wood was nothing more than a quarry, circular, full of stones and bracken, with a few thorns and nondescript saplings, foxholes and rabbit holes. The other was rectangular, mainly a planting of scrub oak trees. Beyond the river smouldered the town like a great heap of blue cinders.

He ran along the top of the first wood and, finding no shelter but the thin, leafless thorns of the hedge, dipped below the crest out of the wind and jogged along through thick grass to the wood of oaks. In blinding rain he lunged through the barricade of brambles at the wood's edge. The little crippled trees were small choice in the way of shelter, but at a sudden fierce thickening of the rain he took one at random and crouched down under the leaning trunk.

Still panting from his run, drawing his knees up tightly, he watched the bleak lines of rain, grey as hail, slanting through the boughs into the clumps of bracken and bramble. He felt hidden and safe. The sound of the rain as it rushed and lulled in the wood seemed to seal him in. Soon the chilly sheet lead of his suit became a tight, warm mould, and gradually he sank into a state of comfort that was all but trance, though the rain beat steadily on his exposed shoulders and trickled down the oak trunk on to his neck.

All around him the boughs angled down, glistening, black as iron. From their tips and elbows the drops hurried steadily, and the channels of the bark pulsed and gleamed. For a time he amused himself calculating the variation in the rainfall by the variations in a dribble of water from a trembling twig-end two feet in front of his nose. He studied the twig, bringing dwarfs and continents and animals out of its scurfy bark. Beyond the boughs the blue shoal of the town was rising and falling, and darkening and fading again, in the pale, swaying backdrop of rain.

He wanted this rain to go on for ever. Whenever it seemed to be drawing off he listened anxiously until it closed in again. As long as it lasted he was suspended from life and time. He didn't want to return to his sodden shoes and his possibly ruined suit and the walk back over the land of mud.

All at once he shivered. He hugged his knees to squeeze out the cold and found himself thinking of the horse. The hair on the nape of his neck prickled slightly. He remembered how it had run up to the crest and showed against the sky.

He tried to dismiss the thought. Horses wander about the countryside often enough. But the image of the horse as it had appeared against the sky stuck in his mind. It must have come over the crest just above the wood in which he was now sitting. To clear his mind, he twisted around and looked up the wood between the tree stems, to his left.

At the wood top, with the silvered grey light coming in

behind it, the black horse was standing under the oaks, its head high and alert, its ears pricked, watching him.

A horse sheltering from the rain generally goes into a sort of stupor, tilts a hind hoof and hangs its head and lets its eyelids droop, and so it stays as long as the rain lasts. This horse was nothing like that. It was watching him intently, standing perfectly still, its soaked neck and flank shining in the hard light.

He turned back. His scalp went icy and he shivered. What was he to do? Ridiculous to try driving it away. And to leave the wood, with the rain still coming down full pelt, was out of the question. Meanwhile the idea of being watched became more and more unsettling until at last he had to twist around again, to see if the horse had moved. It stood exactly as before.

This was absurd. He took control of himself and turned back deliberately, determined not to give the horse one more thought. If it wanted to share the wood with him, let it. If it wanted to stare at him, let it. He was nestling firmly into these resolutions when the ground shook and he heard the crash of a heavy body coming down the wood. Like lightning his legs bounded him upright and about face. The horse was almost on top of him, its head stretching forwards, ears flattened and lips lifted back from the long yellow teeth. He got one snapshot glimpse of the red-veined eyeball as he flung himself backwards around the tree. Then he was away up the slope, whipped by oak twigs as he leapt the brambles and brushwood, twisting between the close trees till he tripped and sprawled. As he fell the warning flashed through his head that he must at all costs keep his suit out of the leaf-mould, but a more urgent instinct was already rolling him violently sideways. He spun around, sat up and looked back, ready to scramble off in a flash to one side. He was panting from the sudden excitement and effort. The horse had disappeared.

The wood was empty except for the drumming, slant grey rain, dancing the bracken and glittering from the branches.

He got up, furious. Knocking the dirt and leaves from his suit as well as he could, he looked around for a weapon. The horse was evidently mad, had an abscess on its brain or something of the sort. Or maybe it was just spiteful. Rain sometimes puts creatures into queer states. Whatever it was, he was going to get away from the wood as quickly as possible, rain or no rain.

Since the horse seemed to have gone on down the wood, his way to the farm over the hill was clear. As he went, he broke a yard length of wrist-thick dead branch from one of the oaks, but immediately threw it aside and wiped the slime of rotten wet bark from his hands with his soaked handkerchief. Already he was thinking it incredible that the horse could have meant to attack him. Most likely it was just going down the wood for better shelter and had made a feint at him in passing – as much out of curiosity or playfulness as anything. He recalled the way horses menace each other when they are galloping around in a paddock.

The wood rose to a steep bank topped by the hawthorn hedge that ran along the whole ridge of the hill. He was pulling himself up to a thin place in the hedge by the bare stem of one of the hawthorns when he ducked and shrank down again. The swelling gradient of fields lay in front of him, smoking in the slowly crossing rain. Out in the middle of the first field, tall as a statue, and a ghostly silver in the undercloud light, stood the horse, watching the wood.

He lowered his head slowly, slithered back down the bank and crouched. An awful feeling of helplessness came over him. He felt certain the horse had been looking straight at him. Waiting for him? Was it clairvoyant? Maybe a mad animal can be clairvoyant. At the same time he was ashamed to find himself acting so inanely, ducking and creeping about in this way just to keep out of sight of a horse. He tried to imagine how anybody in their senses would just walk off home. This cooled him a little, and he retreated farther down the wood. He would go back the way he had come, along under the hill crest, without any more nonsense.

The wood hummed and the rain was a cold weight, but he observed this rather than felt it. The water ran down inside his clothes and squelched in his shoes as he eased his way carefully over the bedded twigs and leaves. At every instant he expected to see the prick-eared black head looking down at him from the hedge above.

At the woodside he paused, close against a tree. The success of this last manoeuvre was restoring his confidence, but he didn't want to venture out into the open field without making sure that the horse was just where he had left it. The perfect move would be to withdraw quietly and leave the horse standing out there in the rain. He crept up again among the trees to the crest and peeped through the hedge.

The grey field and the whole slope were empty. He searched the distance. The horse was quite likely to have forgotten him altogether and wandered off. Then he raised himself and leaned out to see if it had come in close to the hedge. Before he was aware of anything the ground shook. He twisted around wildly to see how he had been caught. The black shape was above him, right across the light. Its whinnying snort and the spattering whack of its hooves seemed to be actually inside his head as he fell backwards down the bank, and leapt again like a madman, dodging among the oaks, imagining how the buffet would come and how he would be knocked headlong. Half-way down the wood the oaks gave way to bracken and old roots and stony rabbit diggings. He was well out into the middle of this before he realized that he was running alone.

73

Gasping for breath now and cursing mechanically, without a thought for his suit he sat down on the ground to rest his shaking legs, letting the rain plaster the hair down over his forehead and watching the dense flashing lines disappear abruptly into the soil all around him as if he were watching through thick plate glass. He took deep breaths in the effort to steady his heart and regain control of himself. His right trouser turn-up was ripped at the seam and his suit jacket was splashed with the yellow mud of the top field.

Obviously the horse had been farther along the hedge above the steep field, waiting for him to come out at the woodside just as he had intended. He must have peeped through the hedge – peeping the wrong way – within yards of it.

However, this last attack had cleared up one thing. He need no longer act like a fool out of mere uncertainty as to whether the horse was simply being playful or not. It was definitely after him. He picked up two stones about the size of goose eggs and set off towards the bottom of the wood, striding carelessly.

A loop of the river bordered all this farmland. If he crossed the little level meadow at the bottom of the wood, he could follow the three-mile circuit, back to the road. There were deep hollows in the river-bank, shoaled with pebbles, as he remembered, perfect places to defend himself from if the horse followed him out there.

The hawthorns that choked the bottom of the wood – some of them good-sized trees – knitted into an almost impassable barrier. He had found a place where the growth thinned slightly and had begun to lift aside the long spiny stems, pushing himself forward, when he stopped. Through the bluish veil of bare twigs he saw the familiar shape out in the field below the wood.

But it seemed not to have noticed him yet. It was looking out

74

across the field towards the river. Quietly, he released himself from the thorns and climbed back across the clearing towards the one side of the wood he had not yet tried. If the horse would only stay down there he could follow his first and easiest plan, up the wood and over the hilltop to the farm.

Now he noticed that the sky had grown much darker. The rain was heavier every second, pressing down as if the earth had to be flooded before nightfall. The oaks ahead blurred and the ground drummed. He began to run. And as he ran he heard a deeper sound running with him. He whirled around. The horse was in the middle of the clearing. It might have been running to get out of the terrific rain except that it was coming straight for him, scattering clay and stones, with an immensely supple and powerful motion. He let out a tearing roar and threw the stone in his right hand. The result was instantaneous. Whether at the roar or the stone the horse reared as if against a wall and shied to the left. As it dropped back on its fore-feet he flung his second stone, at ten yards' range, and saw a bright mud blotch suddenly appear on the glistening black flank. The horse surged down the wood, splashing the earth like water, tossing its long tail as it plunged out of sight among the hawthorns.

He looked around for stones. The encounter had set the blood beating in his head and given him a savage energy. He could have killed the horse at that moment. That this brute should pick him and play with him in this malevolent fashion was more than he could bear. Whoever owned it, he thought, deserved to have its neck broken for letting the dangerous thing loose.

He came out at the woodside, in open battle now, still searching for the right stones. There were plenty here, piled and scattered where they had been ploughed out of the field. He selected two, then straightened and saw the horse twenty yards off in the middle of the steep field, watching him calmly. They looked at each other.

'Out of it!' he shouted, brandishing his arms. 'Out of it! Go on!' The horse twitched its pricked ears. With all his force he threw. The stone soared and landed beyond with a soft thud. He re-armed and threw again. For several minutes he kept up his bombardment without a single hit, working himself into a despair and throwing more wildly, till his arm began to ache with the unaccustomed exercise. Throughout the performance the horse watched him fixedly. Finally he had to stop and ease his shoulder muscles. As if the horse had been waiting for just this, it dipped its head twice and came at him.

He snatched up two stones and roaring with all his strength flung the one in his right hand. He was astonished at the crack of the impact. It was as if he had struck a tile – and the horse actually stumbled. With another roar he jumped forward and hurled his other stone. His aim seemed to be under superior guidance. The stone struck and rebounded straight up into the air, spinning fiercely, as the horse swirled away and went careering down towards the far bottom of the field, at first with great, swinging leaps, then at a canter, leaving deep churned holes in the soil.

It turned up the far side of the field, climbing till it was level with him. He felt a little surprise of pity to see it shaking its head, and once it paused to lower its head and paw over its ear with its fore-hoof as a cat does.

'You stay there!' he shouted. 'Keep your distance and you'll not get hurt.'

And indeed the horse did stop at that moment, almost obediently. It watched him as he climbed to the crest.

The rain swept into his face and he realized that he was freezing, as if his very flesh were sodden. The farm seemed miles away over the dreary fields. Without another glance at the horse – he felt too exhausted to care now what it did – he loaded the crook of his left arm with stones and plunged out on to the waste of mud.

He was half-way to the first hedge before the horse appeared, silhouetted against the sky at the corner of the wood, head high and attentive, watching his laborious retreat over the three fields.

The ankle-deep clay dragged at him. Every stride was a separate, deliberate effort, forcing him up and out of the sucking earth, burdened as he was by his sogged clothes and load of stone and limbs that seemed themselves to be turning to mud. He fought to keep his breathing even, two strides in, two strides out, the air ripping his lungs. In the middle of the last field he stopped and looked around. The horse, tiny on the skyline, had not moved.

At the corner of the field he unlocked his clasped arms and dumped the stones by the gatepost, then leaned on the gate. The farm was in front of him. He became conscious of the rain again and suddenly longed to stretch out full-length under it, to take the cooling, healing drops all over his body and forget himself in the last wretchedness of the mud. Making an effort, he heaved his weight over the gate-top. He leaned again, looking up at the hill.

Rain was dissolving land and sky together like a wet watercolour as the afternoon darkened. He concentrated, raising his head, searching the skyline from end to end. The horse had vanished. The hill looked lifeless and desolate, an island lifting out of the sea, awash with every tide.

Under the long shed where the tractors, plough, binders and the rest were drawn up, waiting for their seasons, he sat on a sack thrown over a petrol drum, trembling, his lungs heaving. The mingled smell of paraffin, creosote, fertilizer, dust – all was exactly as he had left it twelve years ago. The

dilapidated swallows' nests were still there, tucked in the
angles of the rafters. He remembered three dead foxes hanging
in a row from one of the beams, their teeth bloody.

The ordeal with the horse had already sunk from reality. It
hung under the surface of his mind, an obscure confusion of
fright and shame, as after a narrowly escaped street accident.
There was a solid pain in his chest, like a spike of bone
stabbing, that made him wonder if he had strained his heart on
that last stupid burdened run. Piece by piece he began to take
off his clothes, wringing the grey water out of them, but soon
he stopped that and just sat staring at the ground, as if some
important part had been cut out of his brain.

The Harvesting

*'And I shall go into a hare
With sorrow and sighs and mickle care'*

Mr Grooby kept his eyes down. The tractor and reaper below, negotiating the bottom right corner of the narrow, steep triangle of wheat, bumbled and nagged and stopped and started. The sweat trickled at the corner of his eye. Not a breath of air moved to relieve him. A dull atmosphere of pain had settled just above eye-level, and he had the impression that the whole top of heaven had begun to glare and flame.

For nearly three hours, since nine that morning, not the faintest gossamer of cloud had intervened between the sun and the thin felt of his trilby. A sunbather would have escaped to cover an hour ago.

Ten more minutes would finish the field. The best sport of all, he knew, usually comes in the last ten minutes. He would be a fool to go off and miss that after waiting for it, earning it, so to speak, all morning.

Laying his gun over a prone sheaf, he stripped off his waistcoat and draped that beside the gun, then raised his trilby and mopped the bald dome under it with his handkerchief, taking a few steps out and back again to bring the air to some coolness against his brow.

This was surely unnatural heat. He could remember nothing like it. The hanging dust raised by the tractor and the hurrying blade of the cutter absorbed the sun's vibrations till it seemed hot as only a solid substance ought to be. And the spluttering reports, and dense machine-gun bursts from the tractor as it started up the gradient, tore holes in the blanketing air with something fierier and deadlier. Near the edge of the field the dark, scorched-looking figures of out-of-work or off-work colliers, gathering the sheaves into stooks, with their black or tan whippets bounding around them, and one big, white, bony greyhound, appeared hellish, as if they flitted to and fro in not quite visible flames.

This was Grooby's first day out in the open since the previous summer. He had intended to stay out for only a couple of hours, expecting the field to be finished by eleven. Two hours today, four or five tomorrow, and so on, acclimatizing himself gradually, till he could take the whole day and enjoy the whole harvest. Perhaps three hours was a bit too much to begin with; perhaps he was overdoing it.

Ten more minutes then, and he would leave. Ten more minutes and after that, no matter how little of the field was left to cut, he would leave. He didn't want to spoil his holiday at the start.

By standing perfectly still, leaving his body to the sun's rays and shrinking inwardly from all its surfaces, he found he could defy both the slowness of time and the huge enveloping weight of the heat. He crouched in a tiny darkness somewhere near the bottom of his spine and dreamed of his car in the stone barn half a mile behind him across the fields. He smelt the cool leather of the upholstery and the fresh, thickly daubed mustard and beef sandwiches lying there with two bottles of beer under the rug on the back seat.

The tractor came up to make its looping turn at the top corner. As Grooby stepped back, the grizzled chimpanzee figure at the wheel shouted something at him and jabbed a finger down towards the wheat, and the long, dark-brown

creature perched above the cutter shouted and pointed at the
wheat, while the shuddering combination slewed round on
itself, suddenly disgorging its roar over Grooby as if a door had
opened. Then the blade swept in again, wheat ears raining
down under the red paddles of the reaper, every few feet a
new sheaf leaping out on to the stubble – so many activities, so
much hot busy iron, in a wake of red dust, drawing off, leaving
Grooby isolated and surprisingly whole, as if he too had been
tossed out like one of the sheaves.

Roused, he stepped up close and resumed his watch down
the two diverging walls of stalks. The shouts of the farmer and
his man meant they had seen something in the patch. What-
ever remained in there would be whisking from side to side
like fish trapped in shallowing water as the reaper closed in.
Grooby held his gun in the crook of his left arm, like a baby,
fondling the chased side-plates and trigger-guard and men-
tally rehearsing for the hundredth time the easy swing,
overtaking the running shape with a smooth squeeze on the
trigger and follow through – one gliding, effortless motion,
like a gesture in conversation.

Fifty yards behind him, two dead rabbits lay under a sheaf.
He had missed three. His shooting was not good. But he loved
the occasion – or rather, he had looked forward to it, remem-
bering the days last summer when rabbits had been flying out
in all directions, getting themselves snagged in the cutter, or
bowled over by the colliers' sticks, or rolled in a flurry of dust
by the dogs, and he himself shooting to left and right like a
hero at a last stand. That was the sport, banging away.

But last summer there had been no such heat. He wondered if
the farmer thought it unusual. Maybe it was a record heatwave
following the freakish dispersal during the night of some
protective layer in the upper atmosphere. The Sunday papers
would be full of it, with charts and historical comparisons.

Or maybe he was simply growing old, beginning to fail in the trials. He imagined there must be certain little tests that showed the process clearly: a day of rain, the first snow, or, as now, a few hours in the sun. Were these to become terrors? And he had put on a few pounds since last summer.

The trilby was a mistake. His brain felt black and numb and solid, like a hot stone. Tomorrow he would bring a broad-brimmed Panama hat. The stookers would snigger, no doubt, but they knotted handkerchiefs over their heads, like little boys.

He watched the tractor turning again at the bottom of the strip and it was now, as the tractor started up the slope towards him, that a strange sensation came over Grooby. Whether at the idea of all the energy needed and being exerted to drag such a weight of vibrating iron up that hill in that heat, or at the realization that here was help approaching, and he could therefore allow himself to yield a little to the sun, he suddenly lost control of his limbs and felt himself floating in air a few feet above the crushed stubble.

He sat down hastily, adjusting his pose to look as natural as possible, but nevertheless alarmed and with a deep conviction that he was too late. He had closed his eyes and heard a voice in the darkness announcing over and over, in brisk, business-like tones, that he would now leave the field immediately. The sun had gathered to a small red spot in the top of his brain. He thought with terror of the distance back to the farm and safety: the short walk seemed to writhe and twist like a filament over a gulf of fire.

Opening his eyes, he found the tractor's Ford headplate, as it climbed towards him, centring his vision, and like a drunken man he anchored his attention to that as if it were the last spark of consciousness. Slowly his head cleared. He changed his position.

And now, as the world reassembled, he became aware that the farmer was standing erect in the tractor, waving his free arm and shouting. Grooby looked round for some explanation. The stookers had stopped work and were looking towards him, straining towards him almost like leashed dogs, while the dogs themselves craned round, quivering with anxiety, tucking their tails in for shame at seeing nothing where they knew there was something, eager to see something and be off. Grooby took all this in remotely, as through the grill of a visor. He had a dim notion that they were all warning him back from the brink of something terrible. Then his eyes focussed.

A yard out from the wall of wheat, ten yards from Grooby and directly in the path of the tractor, a large hare sat erect.

It stared fixedly, as if it had noted some suspicious detail in the far distance. Actually it was stupefied by this sudden revelation of surrounding enemies. Driven all morning from one side of the shrinking wheat to the other, terrified and exhausted by the repeated roaring charge and nearer and nearer miss of the tractor in its revolutions, the hare's nerves had finally cracked and here it was in the open, trying to recognize the strangely shorn hillside, confronted by the shapes of men and dogs, with the tractor coming up again to the left and a man scrambling to his feet on the skyline above to the right.

So it sat up, completely nonplussed.

Grooby aimed mercilessly. But then he perceived that the farmer's shouts had redoubled and altered in tone, and the farmhand on the cutter had joined in the shouting, flourishing his arms, with violent pushing movements away to his left, as if Grooby's gun muzzles were advancing on his very chest. Accordingly, Grooby realized that the tractor, too, lay above his gun barrels. He held his aim for a moment, not wanting to forgo his prior claim on the hare, and glanced over towards the dogs, flustered and angry. But for those dogs the hare would surely have run straight out, giving a clean, handsome shot. Now, any moment, the dogs would come clowning across the field, turn the hare back into the wheat and hunt it right through and away out at the bottom into the uncut field of rye down there, or round the back of the hill into the other fields.

To anticipate the dogs, Grooby started to run to the left, down the other side of the wheat, thinking to bring the hare against open background. But before he had gone three strides, the hare was off, an uncertain, high-eared, lolloping gait, still unable to decide the safe course or the right speed, till the dogs came ripping long smouldering tracks up the field and Grooby fired.

He forgot all about swing and squeeze and follow through. He was enraged, off balance, distracted by the speeding dogs and at all times hated shots from left to right. But his target loomed huge, close, and moving slowly. The gun jarred back on his shoulder. The hare somersaulted, as if tossed into the air by the hind legs, came down in a flash of dust and streaked back into the wheat.

For a second, Grooby thought he must have fainted. He could hear the farmer yelling to the colliers to call their dogs off, threatening to shoot the bloody lot, but the voice came weirdly magnified and distorted as if his hearing had lost its muting defences. His head spun in darkness. He knew he had fallen. He could hear the tractor protesting on the gradient and it seemed so near, the engine drove so cruelly into his ears, he wondered if he had fallen in front of it. The ground trembled beneath him. Surely they would see him lying there. His sense cleared a little and as at the moment of waking from nightmare to the pillow and the familiar room, Grooby realized he was lying face downward in the wheat.

He must have fainted and staggered into the wheat and fallen there. But why hadn't they noticed him? Twisting his head, he saw what he could scarcely believe, the red paddling flails of the reaper coming up over him. Within seconds those terrible hidden ground-shaving blades would melt the stalks and touch him – he would be sawn clean in two. He had seen them slice rabbits like bacon.

He uttered a cry, to whoever might hear, and rolled sideways, dragging himself on his elbows, tearing up the wheat in his hands as he clawed his way out of the path of the mutilator, and cried again, this time in surprise, as a broad wrench of pain seemed to twist off the lower half of his body, so that for a moment he thought the blades had caught him. With a final convulsion he threw himself forward and sprawled parallel to the course of the tractor.

This is how it happens, his brain was yammering: it can happen, it can happen, and it's happened. This is how it happens. Everything is going nicely, then one careless touch, one wink of a distraction, and your whole body's in the mincer, and you're in the middle of it, the worst that can happen for ever. You've never dreamed it possible and all your life it's been this fraction of a second away, a hair's breadth from you, and here it is, here it is.

The noise of the tractor and the special grinding clatter of the cutter seemed to come up out of the raw soil, taking possession of all the separate atoms of his body. The tractor's outline rose black against the blue sky and Grooby saw the farmer standing at the wheel, looking down. He cried out and waved an arm, like a drowning man, whereupon the farmer pointed at him, shouting something. Then the flails came over, and he heard the blades wuthering in the air. For a second everything disintegrated in din, chaffy fragments and dust, then they had gone past, and Grooby lay panting. Why hadn't they stopped?

They saw him and went straight past. The end of the cutter bar had gone by inches from his face, and now he could see through the thin veil of stalks and out over the naked stubble slope. Why hadn't they stopped and got down to help him? He gathered himself and once more tried to get to his feet, but the baked clods of soil and the bright, metallic stalks of wheat fled into a remote silent picture as the pain swept up his back again and engulfed him.

But only for a moment. He jerked up his head. Hands held his shoulders, and someone splashed his face with water that ran down his neck and over his chest. He shook himself free and stood. As if he had tripped only accidentally, he began to beat the dust from his trousers and elbows, ignoring the ring of men who had come up and stood in a circle watching. All the time he was trying to recall exactly what had happened. He remembered, as if touching a forgotten dream, that he had been lying in the wheat. Had they carried him out then? He flexed his back cautiously, but that felt easy, with no trace of discomfort. The farmer handed him his trilby.

'All right now?'

He nodded, 'Gun must have caught me off balance. Only explanation. Held it too loose. Knocked me clean out.'

He adopted his brusquest managerial air, putting the farmer and his gang of impudent, anonymous colliers' faces back into place. What had they seen, he wondered. They could tell him. But how could he possibly ask?

'One of those flukes,' he added.

The farmer was watching him thoughtfully, as if expecting him to fall again.

'Well, what happened to the hare?' Grooby demanded.

His continued gusty assurance took effect. Whatever they had seen or were suspecting, they had to take account of this voice. The farmer nodded, in his ancient, withered-up way.

'You're all right, then.' He turned on the stookers in surprising fury. *'What the hell am I paying you for?'*

As they all trooped off down the field with their sullen dogs, the farmer started the tractor up and the cutter blade blurred into life.

Left alone, Grooby sank into a shocked stupor. His mind whirled around like a fly that dared not alight. A black vacancy held him. Something important was going on, if only he could grasp it. He seemed unable to move, even to wipe away the sweat that collected in his eyebrows and leaked down into his eyes. It occurred to him that the sun had settled over the earth, so that the air was actually burning gas, depth of flame in every direction. He watched the tractor dwindle in the bottom of the field, as if it were melting into a glittering puddle in the haze. How could men go on working in that temperature? The stookers were clearly charring; they were black as burnt twigs, tiny black ant men moving on the grey field.

One cut up and one down would finish the piece, and this prospect partly revived Grooby, including him once more in events. As the tractor waded up one side – now only fifteen yards or so long – he walked down the other, scrutinizing the thin curtain of stalks where every clump of weeds had ears and seemed to be sitting up alert.

At the bottom, a few paces back into the stubble, Grooby took up his position for the final sweep. Now the hare must either show itself or be killed by the cutter, unless it had already died in there of that first shot. As the tractor bore down, the colliers left their work, edging forward till Grooby noticed they had moved up level with him, as if to supervise the kill. He advanced a little, separating himself. The thought that the hare's first appearance would bring two or three dogs dancing across the line of fire unnerved him. Also, he didn't want these men to be looking at his face, which felt to be ludicrously pink and sweating its very fat.

If only the tractor would hurry up and get it over with or if only the hare would gather its wits and move. But the tractor seemed to have stopped. Grooby blinked and straightened himself vigorously, and that brought the tractor on a little more quickly. From the lowest corner of the wheat the few stalks that would be last to fall leaned out and tormented him in those endless seconds.

Then all at once here was the hare, huge as if nothing else existed. The colliers shouted, and the gun jumped to Grooby's shoulder. But he held his fire. The animal was too near. He saw the roughness of its brindled, gingery flanks and the delicate lines of its thin face. Besides, it seemed to want to surrender, and was so obviously bewildered that for a moment Grooby felt more like shooing it away to safety than shooting it dead. But it had already realized its folly and, swerving sharply to Grooby's right, launched itself up the hill like a dart, a foot above the ground, while the farmer stood shouting in the tractor as those last stalks fell and the dogs behind Grooby climbed the air yelling and coughing on their restrained collars.

He had bare seconds, he knew, before the dogs broke loose all around him, and it was with half his attention behind him that Grooby fired, at ten yards' range. The hare flattened in a scatter of dust, but was on its feet again, flogging its way up the slope, more heavily now, its hindquarters collapsing every few strides. It looked just about finished, and rather than spoil it with the choke barrel or miss it clean, and also in order to be ahead of those dogs whatever happened, Grooby set off at a lumbering run. Immediately the hare picked up and stretched away ahead. Grooby stopped and aimed. The sweat flooded his eyes and he felt he ought to sit. He heard the shouting, and, wiping his eyes and brow with one fierce movement along his left arm, brought his cheek back to the gun as one of the whippets ripped past him like a lit trail of gunpowder. He aimed furiously towards the bounding shape of the hare and fired.

The blackness struck him. The wild realization that he had done it again, the blasted gun had hit him again, was swallowed up.

He seemed to have fallen forward and thought he must have gone head over heels. One need possessed him. It drove him to struggle up the hill. None of his limbs belonged to him any more, and he wondered if he still lay in the wheat and whether the cutter blades had indeed gone over him. But loudest of all he heard the dogs. The dogs were behind him with their inane yapping. He began to shout at them and shouted louder than ever when he heard the sound that twisted from his throat, the unearthly thin scream. Then the enormous white dog's head opened beside him, and he felt as if he had been picked up and flung and lost awareness of everything save the vague, pummelling sensations far off in the blankness and silence of his body.

The Wound

'I came back without a hand, but my comrade was devoured'

FOLK TALE: *Two in Search of Evil*

SERGEANT: Keep going, 521, keep going.

RIPLEY: Keep going !

Does he know where he's leading me, that's the point. What's wrong with him? What's wrong with his walk, for instance? What's wrong with his head? I keep getting that – something wrong with his head. But his head's all right. Look at it. His head's all right. Something wrong with it.

What about me, though, eh? There's me too, isn't there, and am I all right, am I? Is there any answer to that? What's the answer to that? No time in all this, not now, I'll come back to it, I'll catch a quiet five minutes and come back to it at my leisure. Yes, then I'll stretch out! I'll let my fingers forget my hands, my feet forget my driving thighs. I'll let my head go off like the moon and forget. I'll sleep for a thousand years, I'll forget waking. I'll be forgotten.

What went wrong, Ripley? Something's gone wrong. Some thing. A slight error in the thirtieth decimal place is having its consequences – every step a multiplication. Be careful, Ripley.

Now it's up to you, Ripley. You're in a bad way, Ripley. You're tired. What's making you so tired? A leakage of information.

I have red hair. Do you now! Where does that get us?

Nightfall. Nearly nightfall. One flower can still look at

another but night is in the worm's hole. None of this is right, none of it.

Is this the same as what went before, that's the point. That's the puncture. Where's the puncture? Find the puncture. Because if none of this is the same as what went before – is it the same though? This is this. But is it? And even if it were, would I be capable of . . .

I have red wavy hair in one style or another from the crown of my head to the tops of my big toes and I've been that way since I was seventeen and it hasn't cost me a penny, not a penny, in fact I've saved on it. That's the way I am. Was. Shall be. Surely. Can that change? Me, I'm still me. Who's prone? Who's eating earth? Who's forgotten his mouth and eyes?

That sergeant dragging me with an iron ring round my neck and him on a fool's errand without end. Dragging me through this landscape, these seeming locations, and on and on, and I don't want to move.

It's his head that's queer. What's that black mark on his head? Or is it in my eye? It comes and goes. The dusk!

Ripley, you've forgotten something.

You've landed face upward in this world, star-gazer! And what if you do get back home, eh? Even at this rate? You can't sleep there for the blasted clocks!

I'm not myself. Tired. Sarge?

SERGEANT: 521?

RIPLEY: Much farther, sarge?

SERGEANT: Keep going.

RIPLEY: Keep going!

Keep going!

Desert. This desert! Walking through this desert all this time, a desert like raw mustard, a windy desert of raw yellow mustard dust, with an immovable sun like 250 watt bulbs pressed lit on to your eyeballs – walking through this desert accompanied by nothing but your feet and ears, staring not round and about because the mirages are like branding irons, they bear direct on your eyeballs, but staring down at your feet, your boots, going – one after the other, going, carrying you – hour after hour, is it any wonder your brain gets to be – a blister! (*Laughs.*) A great blood blister! Bulging out of your eye-sockets – prick the blebs and it leaks down your face!

If you've got a face.

Ripley! Pull yourself together – you have nothing but your own parts, no spares available, these have to last you to the end. With care, with care! What happened?

After all, this isn't desert. I've never seen a desert. You're here, Ripley. Beautiful soft evening. Lovely midsummer trees. Evening of 22 June, when all the disasters occur. Soft low hills. A lake. That's a heron, gliding. Cool. Take your time. Dew on my boots. Is it dew?

Sarge?

SERGEANT: Keep going, 521.

RIPLEY: But what are we looking for, sarge? I might see it and not know we're looking for it. Eh, sarge!

SERGEANT: Secret orders.

RIPLEY: But who could I tell, sarge? There's nobody else here but you and you know. Don't you? It's getting dark. You might miss it.

SERGEANT: All right. We're looking for a chateau. A white chateau. You know what a chateau is?

RIPLEY: A chateau!

SERGEANT: Keep going.

RIPLEY: A chateau! How does that fit? How does that fit a body abandoned to gravity, at 32 feet per second . . . I'm still here. You're a soldier now, Ripley, a number. If I ever had a home, I'm forgetting it. I'm in the tight black tunnel, like a bullet in the breach, to be blasted into a . . . No, I'm not. Not quite. After all, look at my boots. Boots in grass. Grass, grass, grass – sound of a man moving alive over the open earth, grass, grass, grass, grass! Me? I'm not myself. Exhaustion? Ninety-nine per cent of my brain is sleeping on the march. Am I a zombie, then? One percent awake. That's about one finger awake – one finger twitching, like a man who – (*Yawns.*) There go my boots down there – boot past boot and ahead, leapfrog sidelong. My feet in the boots are travelling asleep, flashing through the grass and countryside in utter darkness, past the copses where the wood pigeons circle down, past the orna-mental lake with its chalet on the island, its statues in the reeds, horsemen, nudes, storks and fauns, past the great oaks over their wells of shadow where the deer flick their ears. My eyes are awake here, travelling horizontally five feet above the grass, through the midsummer twilight. Past the great top-heavy oaks, the elms, the chestnuts, the towering trees at anchor, in a misty harbour, by a still sea, waiting, moored by gossamers to the tips of the grass blades. Trees weighing hundreds of tons of darkness. When the gossamers part they'll float the whole green loaded world away into evening, the deer stirring, the statues pointing, the pigeons sitting side by side in the dark yews, like loaves sliding into an oven – a top-heavy world slowly tilting over into darkness.

Ripley. You're Ripley. Not to forget it. You're the memor-able Ripley.

Who's that young chap walking through the parkland with Sergeant Massey? Oh, that's Private Ripley, you know him.

Private Ripley, you're a fine figure of a lad, you must weigh twelve stone. Thirteen stone six, sir, stripped to the hairs. Well now, can you identify this one? Red wavy hair, sandpaper skin, a birthmark like a bilberry here behind the left ear, prominent nostril hairs, some grey in spite of his youth, large nose twice broken and giving out a click on manipulation, eyebrows recently burned off, eyes – indeterminate, one gold-filled molar, massive neck, heavily freckled forearms the thickness of a racing cyclist's thighs? Hm? Who? Oh, that looks like Private Ripley, sir, in fact it's him for certain.

Me. Ripley, in power. With a headache. Walking.

SERGEANT: Now we bear left.

RIPLEY: Bear left? What does he know about it? I saw him. He staggered to the left, then shouted, 'Bear left.'

Watch him. Where is he? Where is he? Sarge! Sarge! Sarge!

SERGEANT: (*Very close*) I'm here, 521, what's up?

RIPLEY: Where were you? I thought you'd dropped down a hole.

SERGEANT: Me dropped down a hole? Wake up, Ripley, wake up. And hurry up. Bear left.

RIPLEY: (*To himself*) It was different. We were – not here. Was it even summer? I don't think it was even summer. Yes, that's a question now, isn't it, was it even summer, because this is summer.

Exhaustion. When you're exhausted as I am your brain sort of decomposes temporarily, it no longer fills its circuits, like a fountain turned down. Or turned off.

Rain! That was it – rain! It was raining. I was wet. It was streaming, it was dam-burst, mud and rumble and brown water, my uniform was like a dead skin, I couldn't get out of it, and no leaves, there were none of these leaves, the trees were leafless, what there was of them, and there was little enough, they were stumps, stakes, spits and jags – it was forest-fireland, a black downpour moonland, and we were in that farm, we were in that farm, we were in that farmhouse and three tanks, yes, that was it – we were in that farmhouse and Joe Moss – Joe Moss was smashing tops off beer bottles against a brick . . . Wait a minute, wait a minute, get it right. Joe Moss had just had his hand blown off and the blood shot like pop

94

out of a bottle and the rain was hosing down. (*Laughs.*) I've got it, I've got it, it can't get away. (*Shouting.*) That was it, I've got it . . .

SERGEANT: Hold on, boy, hold on. Everything's all right.

RIPLEY: (*Yelling*) I've got it –

SERGEANT: Yes, yes, you've got it and very nice it is now just – there. You're not the first I've seen go off like that.

RIPLEY: (*Normal tone*) What's up, sarge?

SERGEANT: Nothing, boy, everything's fine.

RIPLEY: Look.

SERGEANT: What?

RIPLEY: Water. A stream!

SERGEANT: Was that there? It's all right though, it looks nice and shallow. You know how I know? The path goes straight down to the edge, which means everybody must cross here, which means it must be specially shallow.

RIPLEY: It looks black and deep, that water. Is it water?

SERGEANT: Come on, let's be over.

RIPLEY: Wait a minute. Did you notice how everything suddenly got darker just then?

SERGEANT: What's up with you, 521? Are you all right? You're that pale your face is shining like a lamp.

RIPLEY: That's funny. Your face is all dark and dusky. I can hardly see it.

SERGEANT: I'm not a pale man, that's why.

RIPLEY: (*To self*) I can't see it at all.

SERGEANT: I'm a high-coloured healthy bloke. Are you coming?

RIPLEY: We're being watched.

SERGEANT: Eh?

RIPLEY: Far side, near the top of that grassy slope. See her? She's watching us.

SERGEANT: She?

RIPLEY: It's a woman. It moved.

SERGEANT: You sure it's a woman? Could be a cow tail-end on in this light. Or a post. An owl flew up on to a post to watch us.

RIPLEY: It's a woman. Call to her. Go on, ask her where the chateau is. Try it.

SERGEANT: Hello, Missus, could you direct us to the chateau, please? Could you direct us to the chateau? Something's wrong with your brain, 521. There's nothing there. There's not even a post.

RIPLEY: She vanished. She vanished as you spoke.

SERGEANT: Oh, come off it, Ripley. First I've disappeared when I'm here, then there's some woman where there's nothing, then she's disappeared from where she wasn't – what's up with you? Is there a woman there or isn't there? How are the facts?

RIPLEY: There isn't

SERGEANT: Right. Now cross and no more funny business.

RIPLEY: Maybe the chateau's up this way, sarge. We don't want to cross over only to have to come back, do we?

SERGEANT: Cross. Orders.

RIPLEY: What if you cross, sarge, and I go searching up this way this side of the stream . . .

SERGEANT: 521, we're crossing. Follow me.

He enters, wading.

RIPLEY: It's icy. My feet are going dead.

SERGEANT: Keep going.

RIPLEY: Sarge, it's –

They shout. Great splash.

SERGEANT: All right, boy?

RIPLEY: It's up to my chin and I'm on tiptoe. There must be a trench or a hole or –

Another splash and shout.

96

SERGEANT: Swim for it, boy, the bottom's gone. Swim for your life.

The sergeant pulls himself ashore.

All right, boy, catch my hand. (*Hauls out Ripley.*) That was a surprise. How are we, Ripley?

RIPLEY: Oh, God, it must be snow water. It's frozen my guts in a lump.

SERGEANT: Don't be so soft, man, it's only a bit of water.

RIPLEY: My calves are in knots.

SERGEANT: Here, give 'em a rub. Better?

RIPLEY: It needn't have been like that.

SERGEANT: Can you move?

RIPLEY: Didn't it get you, sarge, at all?

SERGEANT: Didn't seem to touch me. Bit of a chill. Passed in a flash. It was a surprise all right though, who'd have thought, eh? Drowned a few fleas maybe. What's up, 521? What's up? What are you staring at?

RIPLEY: Shh! Behind you. Top of the bank.

SERGEANT: Well, I'm blessed!

RIPLEY: And farther over to the left.

SERGEANT: Another. Are they women? They look like women. But there's something funny about them. (*Calling.*) Hello there, Missus, hello! Could you tell us the shortest cut to the chateau, could you tell us the shortest cut –

As he speaks, one of the women laughs, the other laughs – laughs repeated in the distance. Silence. A groan. Silence.

RIPLEY: (*To self*) Who's this lying here? The boot toes are tilted apart and the feet in them don't seem to care. His boots are here like a load of old surplus, dumped, not caring, no pride, carrying on, good as ever. Here's an ankle with these boots. Another ankle. What else? Search. A hand! Empty, like a beggar's, so weary he has to rest his knuckles on the earth as he begs, waiting for whatever heaven might think to let fall, even if it's only rain. Where does this arm go off to so purposefully? A chest. And over the chest to another arm like itself, sloping away to another hand with upward hooking fingers away there in the distance. This lot looks valuable. Somebody lost it? Somebody going to come back for it? A neck. Throat unshaven. Negligence. Neglect is evident throughout. A neck just thrown here in the muck. Somebody's sole and irreplaceable neck, just lying here. Necks! Necks bent glowing under barbers' razors, necks being sledge-hammered in wrestling rings, necks being fumbled and kissed in dark rooms and dim hallways, in shop doorways, empty churches and under bridges and in train compartments and on office stairs. Necks! Search among them. Necks holding their heads up to cinema screens, necks with boils, necks with cricks, necks bunched sweating pork-fat over strangling collars, necks quivering to the creak of cutlery, necks soaring inaccessible over stoles – search among them, count them out. Finished. This neck's not there. This neck's nowhere among them. A neck's got lost. Is this it?

With the head on it – the face! The hills on their way to other hills negotiate this small broken pasture where the weather works, small cultivated pasture, small signature of man on the crumbling map of clay bad for retaining impressions, this nose, these teeth that seem to have bitten through hot iron, the lips peeled back over wires, this chin pushing up through the earth's crust, swelling up through the web of earthquake, irresistibly joyful mushroom, dragging its hair out of the depths, forcing its brow into the light, a blunt wedge. And the weather works at it enormously, invisibly, a sky-size smith labouring with a hammer of nothing or perhaps everything, though so far there's no change to be seen, the blows are so vast and skilful. That finger is flickering. That finger away down there on that hand is flickering. It's signalling. It's signalling to the stars – hoping they'll pick up some of its code and some of its SOS and in turn might think to signal to the cities. It flickers. It flickers. It lies still.

(*Shouts.*) Sarge!

SERGEANT: OK, 521. We're nearly there. That's it. See it? Lovely sight!

RIPLEY: The chateau! It's all lit.

SERGEANT: No, it's not lit. It's gathering the last light of the sky on its white walls which might be slightly phosphorescent, though why I can't say.

RIPLEY: Look at those lawns. What a setting for a peacock! Look at all those yew trees: they've been barbered into shapes.

SERGEANT: Eagles, swords, crowns and angels.

RIPLEY: All in black living yew! Sarge.

SERGEANT: What?

RIPLEY: Everything's so still!

SERGEANT: Follow me. Forward.

RIPLEY: It's a ruin! He's leading me up to this place as if it were something important and it's a complete ruin. Where are the windows? Those are just square holes. What's that smashed gap over the main entrance? You could drive a tank through it. A direct hit, dead centre! This is a chateau in its last stages, a war-dropping, largely dispersed to the four corners and the remainder going fast.

SERGEANT: As you'll see, the war's been here before us. It swept over and partly through. A once noble approach is a dump of rubble. Step with care. Probably one shell did this.

RIPLEY: Does anybody live here, sarge?

SERGEANT: What do you think?

RIPLEY: It's too quiet for my liking. What do we do now?

SERGEANT: We knock.

RIPLEY: Well, go on, knock.

SERGEANT: Listen.

RIPLEY: What?

SERGEANT: It's not more than once in a lifetime you hear a silence as deep as this.

Laugh in the distance.

What was that?

RIPLEY: What? I didn't hear anything. Was there something, sarge?

SERGEANT: What's that you've got?

RIPLEY: An owl.

SERGEANT: Dead?

RIPLEY: It was lying here on the steps.

SERGEANT: Dead?

RIPLEY: That's queer.

SERGEANT: What is?

RIPLEY: It's head's gone. And it's still warm.

SERGEANT: Still warm? I don't like that. Let's feel.

Wail, far off.

Listen. Did you hear that?

RIPLEY: What, sarge, what's –

SERGEANT: Shh!

RIPLEY: (*Whispers*) What's going on, sarge, what's going on?

SERGEANT: Keep still. Keep still.

RIPLEY: What's happening? My – My – Sarge! Sarge! Sarge! I can't –

SERGEANT: Oh, Jesus Christ, spare us.

Faint yap in the distance, repeated, comes closer.

It's coming right up. Can you see anything, 521, can you see?

RIPLEY *sobs as the yap becomes loud and close, drowning his sobs, till he screams.*

RIPLEY: Sarge!

Yaps cease instantly.

SERGEANT: It comes right up. It came right between us. It

came right up these steps between us. What was it?

RIPLEY: What was it?

SERGEANT: It wasn't anything. It had no body. I was looking straight at it. It was five feet above the ground – just that barking, floating in nothing.

RIPLEY: Let's get back, sarge. This is no place.

SERGEANT: (*Banging on the door tremendously*) Is anybody inside there?

Bangs again.

Is anybody alive in there?

Silence.

I'll raise their blasted dead.

Banging.

RIPLEY: Sarge, the door's opening.

Scrape of door opening.

QUEEN: Good evening. You're expected.

SERGEANT: Ah! Good evening. I'm – er – I'm sorry we had to knock so hard, it's sort of – quiet. Well, if we're expected – it's very nice. Well, that's all right if we're expected. We didn't expect –

We thought, you see –

I'm on secret orders and it's a bit difficult to – to –

This is Private Ripley.

QUEEN: Enter.

SERGEANT: Our boots are a bit dirty.

QUEEN: That was anticipated. Aren't there more of you?

SERGEANT: Oh, yes, you'll get them along all right. They'll be here, they're –

QUEEN: Straight ahead. The banquet's prepared.

SERGEANT: Banquet?

QUEEN: Straight ahead.

RIPLEY: Hey, sarge. (*Whispering.*) What's going on? What's going on, sarge?

Baying and snarling and howling of dogs, a dense pack, screeching and squealing of pigs.

Sarge, explain a bit, hey, sarge!

His voice is drowned by the animals. Uproar of animals becomes mingled with shrieking laughter of women, turns wholly into shrieking laughter that is now suddenly hushed, with a few spluttering titters.

WHISPER: Here they come.

RIPLEY: Sarge, what's this we're walking into, eh, sarge?

WHISPER: Shhh!

RIPLEY: After all, sarge, this is all fancy phoney regalia, isn't it? All this historical pageantry stuff. What's she? Cleopatra the green mummy, what's she all painted up for? I think we're in on an elaborate trap – she's probably a slim officer, it's probably a new commando stunt –

WHISPER: Shhh! (*Silence.*)

QUEEN: The guests. First guest?

SERGEANT: I'm Sergeant Massey, five foot eleven by twelve stone eight, professional infantryman, loving life, liking love, a loafer, no sins but a blank circle where my mother was, no conscience but a mouthful of oath where my father was, chiefly failing in forgetfulness but untroubled by that, concerned chiefly to feed and be cheerful, especially to feed. What is this world? I ride on the bowsprit of five seconds alas, my wake is not my care. It's world enough. My twelve stone eight is just five seconds thick. What is this world, five seconds thick? Who am I to judge of its distinctions, draw up claim and counter claim? I am loaded with vegetables and bullocks and my answer is no questions. My hand is my own. My foot is my own. I am –

RIPLEY: Sarge! Sarge!

WHISPER: Shh!

QUEEN: Finish.

SERGEANT: I am –

RIPLEY: Hey, sarge!

WHISPER: Shh!

QUEEN: You are – finish

SERGEANT: Yours.

Outburst of excitement. QUEEN *raps for silence.*

QUEEN: Second guest?

RIPLEY: Me?

QUEEN: Carry on.

RIPLEY: Carry on what?

WHISPER: Introduce yourself.

QUEEN: Some of these ladies can't see you too clearly.

RIPLEY: I'm Private Ripley.

WHISPER: More.

RIPLEY: 1059521, of the forty-third.

QUEEN: You! What are you doing here?

RIPLEY: I came – with Sergeant Massey.

SERGEANT: He came with me.

QUEEN: Do you know where you are?

RIPLEY: No, but I'd –

QUEEN: Hosts!

FIRST WOMAN: They took me with blood dripping off my chin, my mask was blood and went back over my ears and I'd pulled blood up past my elbows and so I was! And they dragged me from the mob and into the police station, two constables, my toes slapping the steps.

SECOND: The coroner attended, fifteen medical specialists of assorted interests.

THIRD: Experimental psychologists of four countries.

FOURTH: Zoologists of five.

FIRST: Bacteriologists of eight.

SECOND: Anthropologists of seven.

THIRD: With a stuffing of sundries, students and attendants.

FOURTH: While the zinc bench on which they stretched me trembled with the thunder and enthusiasm of the journalists under the windows.

FIRST: They stretched me silently, they accused.

SECOND: Bald domes glistened.

THIRD: Grease oozing among the hair-roots.

FOURTH: Upper lips lifting, quivering.

FIRST: Scalpels descending, quivering.

SECOND: What couldn't they expect?

THIRD: Why, every year dozens disappear, without trace, without a finger-nail or loose hair, and these white jackets already had my canines, roots too, reposing in formalin and I was an extremely interesting case.

FOURTH: Something of an oddity but significant, highly significant.

FIRST: Hardly our type and questionably human.

SECOND: An atavism intact, from the Triassic.

THIRD: And a very curious instance.

FOURTH: My hippopotamus belly was not concealed in the dailies and beside it a list of large-type queries.

FIRST: Vox populi indignation.

SECOND: Portraits of the vanished.

THIRD: Indications to observe well the elephantine distension of my abdomen.

FOURTH: This sack of gorilla gut was not got gnawing carrots, they cried, and they sliced it.

FIRST: With joy.

SECOND: To numbers.

THIRD: To the tower guns.

FOURTH: In the name of the law not to speak of humanity.

FIRST: With the sanction of the queen and twelve grey heads selected in the street at random.

SECOND: They sliced me.

THIRD: Under intense illuminations, they were not in the dark, they did not brave the interior unprepared, their eyes followed their fingers inward.

FOURTH: And what did they find, did they find what they hoped for?

FIRST: Lusted for.

SECOND: Sliced me for.

THIRD: Did they find the gold teeth.

FOURTH: The plastic gums.

FIRST: The glass eyes.

SECOND: The steel skull-plates.

THIRD: The jawbone rivets.

FOURTH: The rubber arteries.

FIRST: The rings.

SECOND: The remains of their darlings.

THIRD: The toe-nails.

FOURTH: The gall-stones.

FIRST: The ear-rings.

SECOND: The hair-pins.

THIRD: The ear-plugs.

FOURTH: The balls of grey hair and the indigestible soles of the feet of all their vanished mysteriously beloved –

FIRST: And after all that what did they find in my mundiform belly? What did the committee of investigation and public security find? They found three gallons of marsh gas and a crust of bread!

Howls, shrieks of laughter. QUEEN *raps. Silence.*

RIPLEY: Sarge –

WHISPER: Shh! (*Silence.*)

QUEEN: This first night's entertainments are prepared. We begin with – the banquet.

General excitement, subsiding instantly.

After this we pass on to – fun and games.

Giggles and squeaks, louder but suppressed instantly.

After that – to the dance.

Exclamations – 'The dance!' etc. Excitement has to be quelled by the QUEEN *rapping.*

Finally – to sleep. (*Silence.*) Will that be suitable, sergeant? You can't refuse, I'm afraid.

SERGEANT: This is – it's – Well, as a matter of fact we were thinking more in terms of an old outhouse, you know, mud floors, animals, creepy-crawlies in your ears, that's more our point of view. But this – I'm speechless.

QUEEN: You're hungry. Your mouth's open.

SERGEANT: I could eat a dead horse.

QUEEN: Nothing here but peacock, snipe, woodcock, quail, black-cock, gamecock and cock starlings. Dogfish, catfish and assorted shellfish. Cod and conger, gudgeon and sturgeon, pickled, creamed or else plain. As you please. Eels. Fourteen kinds of duck, a hare, a boar and a roebuck. To your places. Eat.

VOICES: Sit, here, sergeant, with me.

Between us, sergeant. (*Etc.*)

RIPLEY: (*To self*) And what about me?

See me dying anyway to get sucked in here as if I couldn't see what it was. Lousy old brothel, all tarted up, that's all it is, I can see that. Straight off. Is it though? It's not right, whatever it is. Something's not right.

And what was that funny sort of look she gave me, eh? Explain that. What was I supposed to do, what was I supposed to be, eh? I didn't seem to fit.

Something's wrong with that Sergeant Massey, he's been off all night, he's probably cracking. And look at him now. What's his mouth hanging open like that for? Letting those horrible tarts put things in it – ugh!

Stupid lot of fancy dress all this, that's all it is. She's no more a duchess or whatever than I'm a dustbin. Under all that mass of glittering stuff, she's nothing. Look at her sweating under that load of lousy hair – the lengths they'll go to! Easier just to hang a flag out. Just an old very used up tart under it all. Her eyes go off sideways. Her mouth doesn't fit her face, she can't keep it shaped. She has a neck like a stuffed lizard. Her finger-nails are black.

You're in it though, Ripley.

Dying for a fag and they shove all this stuff at me – birds gone black, fish curling their ends up, fumigants not food.

Laughter.

He's at it though, isn't he? Oh, just look at old Massey there making his bed.

Sleep's all I need, cure me. A bed. Just a bed. One bed. One bed somewhere out of the way. Bloody voices! Just listen! Can-openers.

Don't listen, Ripley, don't look, you don't have to, you can just sit here and let them forget you, just sit thinking, you've plenty to think about, Christ, yes, haven't I? If I weren't to think about – (*Yawns.*)

Rain. I was at rain. Somebody hurt. What was it? I got that. I see. I see. Yes, I see now. This isn't dew on my boots after all.

QUEEN: Silence.

Silence.

Boy. Boy?

RIPLEY: Would that be me?

QUEEN: You're not eating.

SERGEANT: Come on, Ripley, for Christ's sake show some manners, you're not in your mammy's kitchen now . . .

QUEEN: Eat.

RIPLEY: I can't eat fish. It – it makes my feet go dead.

VOICE: Feet go dead? Fish?

QUEEN: There's red meat. Eat.

RIPLEY: I'm a vegetarian. Meat makes me dream blood, it gives me guilt nightmares, I get nightmares being eaten by bulls –

QUEEN: Pass him the gherkins. Eat.

RIPLEY: Not vinegar, it gives me green skin, it loosens my teeth, it makes my hair drop out, it withers all my skin up, it brings me out in fungus –

QUEEN: Eat. Eat.

RIPLEY: I'm eating.

QUEEN: Carry on.

Murmur returns: laughter.

RIPLEY: Madhouse. And I'm one of the worst. I'm really in it. These gherkins aren't so bad though. How in Christ's name did you get into this, Ripley? And what is it, what is it?

Just look at these whores, faces like earwigs, magnified lot of earwigs. Maggots, writhing, squirming to split their seams – carnivorous pile of garbage if ever there was one. Ugliest pack of bitches I ever did see. That was a funny turn they put on. They learn them off records, amuse customers. Look at Massey, though, eh. He's away.

I'll sneak out of this any minute, sneak out and find a dark room, nice and dark and quiet. Then I'll sleep that long sleep.

GIRL: Come with me.

RIPLEY: Were you speaking to me?

GIRL: Come with me, now, quick.

RIPLEY: I'm all right here, thanks.

GIRL: You'd better come.

RIPLEY: Stop pulling. Can't you see: I'm eating gherkins.

GIRL: Put them down.

RIPLEY: Fingers off.

GIRL: Put them down and come with me.

RIPLEY: No, thanks, I know what's good for me.

Jar smashes.

You little bitch! They were my gherkins. You've smashed my gherkin jar. Get out. Clear off.

My boots covered with blood and now my hands covered and Christ knows, Christ knows . . .

Rain. That's what I need, rain. This place is too hot. This place is airless. This place is like a tomb in a desert.

She can't have been more than fifteen. And accosting like a desperate sixty-year-old. Little cradle face, it's amazing how it doesn't show even though it's supposed to and even though it does when they get that greasy look at the mouth corners, or where does it show? Something out of sight like a dog-whistle that gets on your nerves and you can't hear a thing.

Something for all tastes in this place. Not for me though. Ripley's bitch-proof. Ripley's dog-poison. Ripley's going to sit here quietly thinking. Explain a few things. Just sit quietly and explain that blood on your boots because it looks fresh.

Burst of laughter.

WOMAN'S VOICE: No! No! You couldn't.

SERGEANT: Couldn't? Sergeant Massey couldn't? The phrase doesn't exist.

WOMAN'S VOICE: You ate them! Ate them!

SERGEANT: Oh, Lizzy, now, come on, you've trapped mice in your time, what about it?

WOMAN: Ate them though! I get the shivers when I –

SERGEANT: Well, just look at the facts. There we were. Three of us. Three. Not four, not sixty. But three. It was an old farmhouse. Instead of the kitchen we now had a burned-out tank with men hanging down like smoking Christmas trimmings – stopped by this hand. Instead of roof we had sky, full of ghosts just beginning to smell. Instead of floor we had mud and the remnants of friends. Instead of a view we had quag, leafless quag. Between three of us – two Lewis guns. No food. Plenty of ammo. No food. Rain battering down. Three full-utility fighting men, unscratched. I alone, I alone must have accounted for well over, well, say at a guess, four hundred of the enemy. Don't stare, think of it. Count it up. One, two three, you, you and you – bang, bang, bang – four hundred. It takes time. It takes a kind of care. All this time no food. How did we fuel all this personal zest? Were we to be wasted, starved – put under not a new wave of the enemy, resisting formidably, but a miserable hermetic pang in the gut! Principles! Principles came to our aid.

Imagine. These strong lads underfoot – sacks of home-fed weren't they? Oh now, now, now. When you've shot one man into individual bite-size pieces, no ancient prejudice remains whole – everything's holes, anything's holy, if it serves. They served. We served them. Why, what would their mothers think, us leaving their boys trodden under that five square yards of undistinguished terrain in neglected postures? Better that we say: 'Lady, I took your son into my own blood and brought him back alive though, alas, killed, but alive . . .'

Shrieks and 'Ahs' and 'It's so exciting'.

At the last ditch – and it was a ditch and it was the last – with our guns burning a hopeful circle of survival – for us – like a gas-ring, round us, and the enemy, unnumbered, clutched at the slippery clouds and bellyflopped into the quag, well, look, I'll give you the facts. We cut up those dead lads of ours and ate them raw.

Shrieks, squeals.

RIPLEY: Sarge!

SERGEANT: You were there, Ripley, don't look so righteous.
Excited murmurs and cries: 'Tell us more, tell us more. What next?' 'You're so brave!' and 'That takes real courage'.

Courage? Don't speak to me of courage. As if all that hadn't been enough, we seemed by chance and misfortune to lie right in the next wave of not men. They'd got fed up sending men into that porridge. No, tanks we got next, tanks, in waves. Crawling at us, sawing away at us and fuming and cursing, and at other blokes too, you know, we weren't alone quite in this war. Have you ladies ever seen a tank head on, waddling at you, spraying you with red-hot zinc dust and flying earth? No, I know you haven't. Three of us. Flesh and blood. What could we do? Surrender? How? Wave our vests? They were black. So how did we end it? How did we go under? In what way did we die?

RIPLEY: Sarge!

SERGEANT: In what way did we die?

GIRL: (*Whispers*) Come now, quick. Quick.

RIPLEY: Sarge!

SERGEANT: Joe Moss went first. He jumped erect in our pit and started blazing away blindly like a roman candle and that was an expression of his youth rather than of his good sense. But of course he hadn't stood like that ten seconds, not ten seconds, when he went suddenly all calm and still and philosophical – you could see in a flash his face had changed completely. He held his arm up to show us that the hand had vanished. What do you expect? And while he stood like that – well, it's hard to say.

GIRL: (*Whispers*) Quick, now, come.

WOMEN'S VOICES: More, more, give us more. We can't have enough of it. Give it to us. Let's have it all, to the end, to the end. More, more!

SERGEANT: I went next. I wasn't so premature as Moss, but I didn't mourn him long. While he was still moving, a shell hit me here, on the point of the chin. You couldn't see me for mud.

Rising voices drown his – shrieks.

GIRL: Now, now, now.

RIPLEY: What are those women doing to the sergeant?

GIRL: Come with me, come with me.

RIPLEY: Sarge!

GIRL: Leave him. He's finished. Hurry, hurry, hurry. In here, in here.

RIPLEY: What sort of a rat-hole's this? It's pitch black. Where's the light, let's have some light.

GIRL: Shh! Be still. Hold me.

Silence.

RIPLEY: (*Bursting out*) I can't leave Sergeant Massey like that. Did you see what those women were doing to Sergeant Massey? One of those women had Sergeant Massey by the hair. One had his leg between her thighs and was trying to twist his foot off. His arms were out of their sockets. What sort of women are they, are they women?

GIRL: Shh. Be still. Kiss me.

Silence.

RIPLEY: (*Outburst*) What's this place? Why have we come into this room? Why is it pitch black? Where's the –

GIRL: (*Stopping his mouth*) Shh. Hold me. Harder.

Silence.

RIPLEY: (*Quiet*) Did you see the blood? Did you see all the blood?

GIRL: I saw it.

RIPLEY: (*Whispers*) Who are you?

GIRL: Hold me. Hold me. Hold me.

RIPLEY: What is it?

GIRL: There he goes, there he goes now.

SERGEANT MASSEY'S *voice comes yelling towards them, with a pounding of feet, shrieking laughs of women. Feet and shouts rush past, as if through the room, and away like lightning into the far parts of the house, culminating in a long shriek of* MASSEY'S *followed instantly by dead silence.*

GIRL: (*As* RIPLEY *begins to blurt something*) Shh.

Silence.

RIPLEY: He's been murdered. Sergeant Massey's been murdered. He's been murdered by those lunatics and you've been keeping me in here out of the way and no doubt it's my turn next. Get your arms off me, you sly little bitch, off. Sergeant Massey's been murdered, while I –

GIRL: Don't push me away. Don't push me away. I love you, I do, I love you, I don't want to leave you, don't push me away. Hold me. Kiss me. Love me, love me.

RIPLEY: Get away, get out! Shut up. Shh! I want to listen.

GIRL: Love me.

RIPLEY: Will you shh!

GIRL: Hold me.

RIPLEY: Look, are you a half-wit? You looked quite intelligent out there, have you gone crackers since? Do you have mild fits and funny half-hours or what? Did you hear what I heard? Did you? Are you still there?

GIRL: Yes.

RIPLEY: Right, then get out of my way, because I'm going through that door when I can find it. Will you do as I say and get your hands off. (*He throws her away. She cries out, hurt.*) What did you expect? Where's that door? Is there a door?

GIRL: Wait a minute. I've something to tell you.

RIPLEY: Where's that door?

GIRL: I've something to tell you.

RIPLEY: No doubt.

GIRL: You've been shot, you know.

RIPLEY: What?

GIRL: You've been shot through the head. I thought you might as well know. You've a terrible bullet hole right through your head. (*Silence.*) There's a place where it went in and a place where it came out and a tunnel between.

RIPLEY: What? What? (*Silence.*) What did they say? Where

are you, you girl, you, what's your name, where are you? What's that you said?

He blunders about, falls over a chair, cries out in pain.

Shot through the head?

Crazy to say that, crazy to say it. It's just another nut-house remark, I've been hearing them all night. What about Massey? He was here with me large as life, I've been with him all night, I came miles with him over all those fields and parks and trees and lakes and that black icy river and the lawns and he went ahead large as life, large as life, and he was blown to bits absolutely to bits, disappeared in the air – (*Shouts.*) So it's stupid to say I've been shot through the head, something must be wrong with your brain. (*Silence.*) There's nobody but me in this room.

It has padded walls I notice, for the hard cases, you see, just as I thought. Everything's quite simple. This is an asylum for specially hard cases. Now there must be a door because I came in and heard it. There, you see. Everything's normal enough, even here. Quite a nice modern sort of lever-handle. There, and it opens, naturally.

Thick dark as ever. And dead still. That's normal.

Slowly, Ripley. The world is happy. And keep easy. Listen for spiders. The walls, the floor – there's a geographical limit to the size of all these places. There you are, rewards already.

A light. A lantern hanging. Phosphorus. Smell? Stink!

Of all things, a rotten phosphorescent fish hanging on a string, hanging on the hook in fact, just as it was caught probably. What a lantern! Better than a human head hanging without a string. And it's quite practical, after all. It works. It lights up a doorway.

Door clicks, creaks open.

And here we are in the armoury. Or is it a museum? Empty

armours, at attention, loyal St Georges surviving the worm and the virgin, faces open for inspection.

And a candle on a pillar. It glows curiously red. No it doesn't, the candle's not lit. That light comes from the walls, from all over the walls, as if they were faintly crimson, luminous.

Who's this? Sitting, his head in his hands. The Janitor? The nightwatchman, dozing, his head in his hands, his back bent like a man's back bent over the shoulder of a man who has come to rest and kneels and prays. The others listens. Neither moves. They are one.

Sergeant Massey! It's Sergeant Massey! Sarge!

Hey, sarge, wake up, it's me, Ripley. Thank God, I was thinking you'd been pulled to bits by those nutty women.

Hey, sarge.

He's breathing.

Sarge, wake up. I thought they were after you, sarge, I could swear it was your voice, sarge, and I thought they had you too, did you hear that screaming, there was the most terrific scream.

What's he covering his face for? This is the right face, isn't it? It is. It's it. It fought, did this face. Massey carried this face into battle thrust out ahead of his vital parts. What didn't it fight, this face? It fought –

Behind the bomber flights, the dive-bombers, the strafing, the reaping from the air with rockets, the tanks treading, the unsewing machine guns, the big berthas vomiting truck loads of dead high explosive men, the howitzers ploughing and mucking, the field-guns spewing boot-soles and bits of rib, the mortars, haemorrhaging over acres, the flame throwers, the stens, rifles, grenades, mines, the primitive tribes of bombs, bottle bombs, jam-tin bombs, glue bombs, boobies, bear-traps, bayonets, blades of every family and name, with all their bastards and dark horses, maces, francescas, bills, pruning hooks, phlegm, turnips, dead sticks snatched up, half-bricks, gravel, clods, fists and invective –

A face.

A face, arms raised, fingers hooked, gums bared, eyes protectively narrowed.

A flash, and the flesh flies off that face. Then it comes on, the glistening grotesque of bone still comes on. A flash, and the visor, the cheek-plates, the girder ridges, the memorial skull-strakes, scatter to shrapnel. But the naked brain, the stripped, grey, stubborn brain, comes on, like a snail freshly skinned, an airborne medusa jellyfish flickering its electrodes, an ectoplasm elemental, a flying malevolent custard!

He was up against it!

(*Whispers*) Sarge.

His brow is sweating. His eyes are trying to open. They can't.

What have they done to him?

What's he doing here, he was blown to bits?

(*Whispers*) Get out, Ripley, get out.

What?

Get out, get out, get out.

(*Runs shouting*) Get out, get out.

Light, light! Thank God, a place with some candlepower. Oxygen, candlepower, and a concessionary pause in time. Where I can breathe. And look. And think thoughts. What's this? Where I can remember words.

His voice begins to echo as in a large empty hall.

A ballroom. Spaciously planned, graciously adorned. Scarlet curtains from the gilded moulding of the ceiling to the gloss black floor like waterfalls of blood falling from the bedrooms above. I never before saw a floor made completely of black glass. Unscratchable, unlike flesh. An oiled, impregnable beauty, in a sense. Inviolable, by one boot or the other. Simply silica? A black lake, breathless, diamond hard, without mist or fish, where I stand between waterfalls of blood and look down into my reflection, perfect but inverted. Nothing moves.

I feel terrific! This place makes me feel terrific! It's like the top of a mountain, this isn't air, this is ether. You can slide –

He takes a run and slides.

What a slide! This is terrific.

Hello? Company? A gentleman! Excuse me, I'm lost, if you could direct me to the exit . . .

He doesn't answer because he's a dummy estranged from life or the hopes of life. He doesn't answer because all his concentration gathers to keep a needle point of stillness balanced on a needle point of silence, while his violin takes aim on the first far-off, soft, slowly approaching note.

He wears a nice suit I notice, and his carnation is both genuine and fresh. And white. His skin is whiter, shaved within the hour or made of wax. His eye is black. It gleams under its lowered eyebrow like an adder's head in a wall-crevice. It gleams at me, pretending not to.

I see you.

Music. Strike up. Look, you waxwork, I'm skating over your priceless floor with my ironbound blood-sodden boots – give me some music.

He slides. First bar of a waltz. He stops.

What?

All right. Again. Try again. Where's your fiddlestick, you stuffed dummy, I'm raking over your flawless floor at forty miles an hour – that's the way, that's the way!

Violin starts waltz in earnest. Murmur of voices, women and men.

Round and round and round we go.

Murmur grows, orchestra comes in, sounds of a full-scale ball.

SERGEANT: 521, you haven't changed your boots.

117

RIPLEY: Sarge! Hey, sarge, are you here?

MOSS: Eyup, Ripley, you gormless bugger, don't stand round out here like a bloody donkey, folk are dancing.

RIPLEY: Moss! Moss, you're dead.

JENNINGS: This is the life, Ripley, this is the life. Get yourself a slice, there's no shortage and all willing. Look at this – I just got hold of her as I came in and we've been outside twice already.

Voice passes.

RIPLEY: Jennings! That was Jennings. And he died a week ago and the rum I gave him ran back out of his mouth: he had a wound that would have stopped a Bedford truck.

BALDWIN: Out of it, Ripley. What a war, eh? You haven't changed your battle-dress, you silly bloody nitwit.

RIPLEY: Baldwin! Not you too.

SERGEANT: Get those boots changed, Ripley, they're dirtying the floor.

RIPLEY: Sarge!

Now, Ripley, just steady yourself, there's a good lad, just take a grip, because if there's something wrong it's here, it's all here.

(*Shouts*) All of you, all of you stop, stop, you're dancing with a lot of dolled-up earwigs, stop dancing you're full of holes . . .

Dance goes on with slight acceleration.

Sarge! Moss! Baldwin! (*He sobs.*) What is it? What is it? It's your head, Ripley, it's your head. No it isn't, it isn't. I see what it is.

He cries out in pain – dance goes on.

GIRL: Hello.

RIPLEY: You? Hello. You're not dancing.

GIRL: You hurt me.

RIPLEY: This is my favourite waltz. Shall we dance?

GIRL: I can't

RIPLEY: I must have lost my temper. I've a very bad headache and what temper I ever had seems to have leaked away. Can you resist this music?

GIRL: Yes.

RIPLEY: What's behind these curtains? I wonder if there's a moon. It was a nice evening earlier on and it should be nearly dawn. Let's go for a walk outside. Me and you. See the flowers stretching and yawning. See the sun come out of its hole.

What was that you said about my head?

GIRL: Your head?

RIPLEY: Look at my boots. That blood's fresh. It's coming from somewhere.

GIRL: Let's go for this walk.

RIPLEY: I can't. I keep getting this feeling it's raining – I don't like rainy dawns. Besides, when I close my eyes I don't seem able to move.

GIRL: Look. Behind these curtains there are french windows.

RIPLEY: This is a craftily designed place.

GIRL: Look. They open.

Sound of storm, wind, rain and gunfire.

RIPLEY: What's happened to the trees? They were baled up with leaves, they were full of pigeons, they were fat and full and kneeling under the load.

GIRL: They've been combed out, amputated, cleft, clotted together, pushed over, blackened, abandoned, like the hair of a chewed and spat out head.

RIPLEY: Rain!

GIRL: In its fifth week. The valleys are flooding, the lakes and ponds are brown as old blood, the farms are wading, the dead are loosening from the ground, the cattle are bladders lodged in treeforks. Dead dogs float in and out of bedroom windows. Hillsides are beginning to move. Lost men give up in the fields as in mid-Atlantic. Solitaries sail out to the horizon on haystacks.

RIPLEY: What's that great sky-blinking glimmer and the rumble, like the sun trying to rise? I suppose lots of summer thunder goes with all this.

GIRL: That's your life, working at the hole in your head.

RIPLEY: What?

GIRL: That's the war, working at all the undead. Well, aren't we going to walk?

RIPLEY: Me? Walk out there? I'm not a country boy. I'm getting back in. I'm going to dance.

GIRL: I want to walk. I'm going to walk.

RIPLEY: Out there? Under that?

GIRL: I prefer it.

RIPLEY: Then goodbye.

GIRL: (*Cries*) Come with me.

Sudden muffling up of storm sounds, music again.

RIPLEY: Capricious little bitch, wants a romantic walk in the cloud-burst and thinks I'm not about two centuries past it.

Narrow your mind now, Ripley, to essential things.

Keep your head very still so your thoughts can roll accurately down into the right hole.

You're very drunk. In fact, you're soused. You're a drowned rat, Ripley, you disgusting person.

Where did you get the drink, eh?

Where's your party spirit? Come on now, get yourself something nice, follow your nose, it's relaxing. (*Hums waltz.*) That's the way. See, the headache goes when you do what the headache wants to. All psychological. (*Hums.*) This music's a bit fast. No, no, that's your sodden head, Ripley, can't keep up with the world. There now, how about that there, all the trimmings, take that one off, Sergeant Massey.

The Wound

Hums the waltz which now starts to go slower and slower and heavier and heavier. Cries of surprise and protest turn to cries of pain.

What's going on? Why is everybody lying down? I don't know this dance. (*Shouts.*) Stand up, sarge, your legs have collapsed. Baldwin, what's wrong?

Sarge? Look out, Moss, that woman's –

It's these women!

These women are dragging them all into the ground, it's a massacre. No, they're all sinking together in the black glass, it must have melted with their dancing or the floods have got at the cellars, they're all going under with their women round their necks, with their women panicking and choking their efforts. No, no, no, this isn't glass it's mud and those aren't women and they aren't panicking –

Sarge! Sarge! Sarge!

Growing sound of storm, wind and rain, and rumble of thunder of gunfire. RIPLEY *staggers.*

Ripley, Ripley, are you there, Ripley?

Yes, yes, yes, I'm here. We're not alone, we're with ourself. And it's raining like hell but we're here, yes, and this mud's only mud, sweet mud, good earth at other times, mother of mankind.

We're here. Good old Ripley.

In power. With a headache. Can you move? Move. Move your fingers: look – communications intact. The finger – signals perceptibly, even at this distance. Stand a bit. Maybe the blood'll stop and what if it doesn't? I'll take a draught on the bank. Sway, sway, let the wind sway you, Ripley: oak-tree Ripley riding the punches. All that lovely blood going straight into the ground, it'll grow a nice swede there one day, dried blood full of nitrogen, beneficent. There's a lot of rain missing you that would be hitting you if you were walking.

What a night, eh? What a night to be standing on this bastardly globe of mud in this bastardly sluice, waiting for sunrise. It's a bastard. It's not a bus-stop.

The rain's hammering me in. I'll freeze. I'm being driven in like a steel spike. I'll be preserved frozen. They'll come for me after the war, light a fire at my feet. I'll step out fresh, my bed'll be waiting, hot bath, hot-water bottles, hot beer with ginger and brown sugar.

You try moving now, though, just try, just you try, go on, try. I can't

Oh, Ripley, you've really caught it.

GIRL: Come on, I'm waiting.

RIPLEY: That's that girl again.

GIRL: I'm waiting. You can't stay there.

RIPLEY: I'm hurt.

GIRL: Lean on me. Try to walk.

RIPLEY: No, no. What are your shoes like in this mud, I bet they're a sight. My feet are stuck in the mud. We'd better wait till the rain stops.

GIRL: You can walk. You're walking.

RIPLEY: What's your name? Ah, yes, you told me, didn't you. Did you? My memory's been dismantled.

If ever I get back to streets do you know what I'll do? I'll marry you. But we're far out.

I'll marry you. I swear by these boots, by the two holes in my head, entrance and exit, that I'll put my whole body in your bank and you can let me out to myself on an annuity. Will you marry me, though? I'm forgetting, aren't I? That should come first. Will you marry me?

Music ends . . . Pause.

Splashing steps approach.

FIRST SOLDIER: Who's there?

RIPLEY: Old trick . . . Disappeared. You're a nitwit tonight,

Ripley. The world's getting more of a grip on you than you have on it. Is she there? Will you marry me? Don't dazzle there!

SECOND SOLDIER: It's one of ours. Look at that head! He's out on his feet. Get him, got him?

FIRST SOLDIER: Steady . . . You're OK. You're in. It's one of Massey's platoon.

SECOND SOLDIER: Get back and bring a stretcher up, he can't walk with his head.

Steps splash away.

They weren't completely wiped out, then.

FIRST SOLDIER: What's he muttering? He's muttering away here.

RIPLEY: Marry me.

SECOND SOLDIER: Eh? What's that, boy? You trying to say something? What's he smiling at? Look at this, grinning away as if he'd been crowned. He's more like a drunk than a man with that on his head.

FIRST SOLDIER: Can we carry him?

SECOND SOLDIER: Right. Easy, though.

FIRST SOLDIER: He must have walked over nine miles with that lot, straight towards us. That's animal instinct for you. Look out.

SECOND SOLDIER: Bleeding mud. What a rotten morning. OK, I've got him.

FIRST SOLDIER: Keep going.

Their steps splash away in the steady downpour.

The Suitor

I walk slowly up the hill. It is a black night. Cars sizzle past, and the light rain snows through the beams of their headlights. The surface of the road, the pavements, the low walls, the jumbled shrubbery in the cramped gardens, the iron railings, the gates, the puddles, glisten and glitter like coal, as the wind tugs at the street lights. It is after ten. It is December.

I am warmly dressed, and with my hands deep in my raincoat pockets, in gloves, huddle my garments tighter about me. I feel invulnerable, except for my feet: the soles of my black shoes are too thin. They feel like compressed cardboard. I can feel them blotting up the wet. I bought these shoes for dancing, but I have never danced. I have never even gone to a dancing lesson. Now I wear these shoes when I want to feel smart. Clean shoes make a light heart, a proverb I continually prove. Nevertheless, tonight these soles are out of place. I have resigned my feet to their condition. I have retrenched comfort to a point a little above the ankles.

A wind chopping and cutting and swirling in from all directions throws up the boughs of the elms as I pass under the rectory wall, and swipes my lapels against my cheeks, and clogs my hair with the drizzle. It whips my turn-ups. It roars among the buildings, and thuds and bumps in the distance.

Here is the house. A truly commonplace house, semi-detached, pebble-dashed, with a shallow defence of imperishable shrubs. Tonight it is merely one half of a black oblong mass. Oily glints determine the windows. It shows no lights.

By day the gate of this house is a dull sooted green, bearing a small oval sign: 'Please shut this.' Its door and window frames are the same green. The lower window of the front room or sitting-room or parlour preserves a cold morgue darkness from year-end to year-end. It is the room in which they lay out their dead. The upper window, or front bedroom, is sealed from the road by the backs of the dressing-table mirrors. Next door, everything is the same, except for the colour of the woodwork, which is a dull sooted red. Even so, the green here is no distinction. In the twelve houses before the next street it recurs seven times. The red is more distinctive, it recurs only twice. Then there is one house brown, and one house black, uniquely.

I am walking slowly, but now I slow down till I move at no more than a saunter. I have seen clearly that the house shows no lights to the front. Perhaps a light shines from the kitchen or side window, but this is difficult to know, because a high wattle fence, parallel to the front garden wall and the road, joins the side of the house to the side of the next and lower house, concealing the side door and kitchen window and the back garden from view of the road. In this fence there is a flimsy door, on the straight concrete path which leads from the front gate, past an offshoot to the front door, to the side door. It is a path I have never trodden, except in imagination. And the door in the high fence, which I have never opened, is shut. I walk slowly, in order to detect signs of light through the chinks of the wattle.

At this moment I am aware of my attention being drawn forcibly in the opposite direction. Since I am peering towards the wattle from my eye-corner, without any public show of curiosity, with my face set directly ahead and downward a little, I have only to switch my eyes across and I see the figure of a man standing under the wall of the derelict smithy at the bottom of the mud lane, which at that point leads off, an old farm lane, into waste-land and new building sites beyond. For a moment, I make an effort to see him at all, since he stands in the blackest of the cone of shadow protected from the nearest street light by the corner of the stone-built smithy. I detect him as a form slightly lighter than the shadow, and I see or think I see what must be the pallor of a face. Evidently he is in hiding, his feet on the wet earth of the lane. A man merely waiting would surely stand on the pavement, in good light. Why should anyone wait just there, though? Or, more seriously, why should anyone choose just that place to hide?

What other motive should I suspect? I have walked five miles merely to look at this house, merely for the gamble of walking past this gate from which it is her custom to emerge. A calculation that nowhere on earth would I have quite as good a chance of meeting her, even at this hour, as on the fifty yards of pavement either side of her front gate, has brought me five miles with a concentrated mind. The hope of passing her gate at the very moment she chooses to leave her house, and the faint possibility that my hope may be an intuition, one of those precise and practical signals that bring insects over miles, male to female, has brought me this far and at this hour. And have I no rivals?

Is she exclusively my secret? I scarcely know her. I have watched her at a distance, outstanding among three hundred others. Lately, whenever we have met in the school corridors, she has seemed to smile at me. And here I am, hopeful of a beginning. As yet, I have not even spoken to her. So who may he not be? What could he not tell me about her? I see her life may be more formidably rooted than I had cared to anticipate.

I walk up the hill as far as the next side-street, and by now I am convinced that he is in ambush – for her. I cross the street. I turn downhill, walking casually, whistling thoughtfully, walking on the outer balk of the pavement, noting again the working glitter of the gutter as the fine rain drains from the black road. I look into a street light and conclude that this rain, if it were daylight, would seem heavier than it now feels, and would seem much too heavy to be strolling and whistling in. In fact, I now see that it is raining hard. The observation causes me no anxiety.

As I approach the lane I move in towards the inner edge of the pavement, keeping my scrutiny down. I am quite self-possessed, only curious. Not until the last moment, as I draw level with the shadow beside the smithy, do I glance up – as an unsuspecting passer-by might well glance up, catching at the last moment a glimpse of someone concealed in shadow and so close. Immediately, I look down and pass on, and for a while I cannot think what to do, for my suspicions have been confirmed in the intense shock of seeing an utterly white face, under the level brim of a trilby, above the tight gorge of a raincoat buttoned to the throat. A very thin face, it seemed. At such close range, the shadow had not protected him. A very long thin face. What age? He had not been leaning against the smithy wall, but standing clear and in the rain, a foot from it. A face without expression, like the face of a man driving at tremendous speed. He had looked straight at me.

A hundred yards farther down, I stop at the entrance of the rectory drive, in solid shadow, under the spattering, agitated trees. From here, the curve of the road above presents the front of the smithy plainly lit, and I watch the black gap beyond it. I would prefer to be above him, so that I could observe the house too, which is hidden from this point. Rapidly, I set off to correct my disadvantage. A brief detour through avenues and crescents brings me out again at the side-street above the house, and I stroll down three gateways, finally stopping under an overhanging bush, where I feel concealed. I can see the bottom of the farm lane, but no figure: only black shadow. I wait. I will wait here as long as he waits there.

Minutes pass. Cars zip up the hill from the direction of the town, with steaming tyres. The clock beyond the vicarage elms strikes and the chimes fly over nakedly or are muffled away out of hearing as the wind worries them. Eleven o'clock. I hug my garments to me, reshuffling my warmth. Behind me the shrubbery shudders and flinches dismally. I am a black column of patience.

Now it comes to mind that in the minutes between my passing him on my way downhill and my arrival at this position he could easily have left, going either downhill or up. This is an unsettling thought. I had not reckoned on lying in wait for her. To walk past her gate, pleasurably, was all I had wanted. Ought I to move? Ought I perhaps to move down another gateway or two? That would be getting dangerously near, if he is still there.

I will wait here, till the quarter strikes, and if he has not shown himself by then, I will drop the whole business and go home.

I stand.

Lights in the houses opposite go out. One bedroom light there has been burning since I came. The wind jerks and pulls to and fro, and the rain flicks as from a tugged tightrope. Time becomes immeasurably dense and solid, as I begin to feel the patience of the houses and the gardens.

The quarter strikes, concentrating my attention on the black shadow by the smithy. I wait. Now I realize that a figure has already stepped out clear and stands there on the pavement, at the very edge, looking across at her house. I press back into the gate recess, thankful that the house behind me is dark. How amusingly will our situation be reversed if he now crosses the road and walks uphill past me and looks sideways just at the right moment to find me squeezed in hiding here.

I have been ignoring the passing cars. Now a large black saloon coming downhill attracts my notice. It is slowing? It is slowing, and swinging across from its own side with orange signal in evidence, gliding down, gathering the whole darkness to the blood glow of its brake signals and its rocking stop. I watch, as I might watch a bomb that comes to rest from its astonishing arrival, and lies quiet. My whole consciousness fastens upon it.

She is here. I know it, and as doors on both sides open, and the dim inner light comes on, her appearance is no surprise, the great fleece of hair as she straightens under the street lights and slams the door behind her. But who is this other, hurrying around to her side of the car, towering over her, adjusting her collar with such familiarity? Ah, yes! I sink, as it were, into the bottom of my mind. Surely this is no more than I expected? Hardly, since she is not yet sixteen, and that car is of a managerial volume and opulence. I dislike what I see, and what I infer. I hear his voice, confident and unsubdued, as he leads her back around the car and on to the pavement where, as I now see, a third figure has appeared and awaits them.

They are stopped in conversation. Without forethought or design, I drift out of hiding and loiter slowly down towards them, as if I were waiting for someone to catch me up. To support this appearance, I half-turn, pausing to look back up the hill, whistling softly to myself.

The three figures are in alarming activity. She flies to the wall, as if she had been struck. I see her tall partner's arm rising and falling, as if he chopped wood. I see the third figure rolling on the pavement, climbing to his feet, falling again, rising upright and falling again, as the tall man's arm administers over him. All this is twenty yards away, in the harsh cold wet shadows. In a few seconds, without a sound, it is over. The defeated one sits up and settles a trilby back on his head. At once I recognize the watcher from the lane-end. He slews and sits at the kerb, back bent low, as if he were spitting into the gutter. I find I have walked much closer.

The girl and her escort have disappeared. Into the house? Yes, here he is again, coming down the path as I arrive by the gate. He shows no visible signs of excitement, only his hair seems perhaps slightly crested, and the street light gleams on the balding skin beneath it. He is very tall, and his powerfully tailored overcoat, his packing of scarf and great gloves, give him a giant shadow. He glances at me, and I recognize the type of face, I recognize a familiar category of face. Ah, no! I like him less and less, in these seconds. I like what I infer less and less.

He looks around, briefly, up the road and down. I too, in my assumed aspect of passer-by, notice that the extra figure has vanished. As I continue, I hear the gate clack shut and footsteps go back up the path. I walk on, exhilarated and calmed by what I have seen in simply strolling down thirty yards of pavement. Involuntarily, as if to anchor this extraordinary occasion more surely in its setting, I look across the road to the smithy.

The watcher is back in position, in the shadow.

I look ahead sharply, like one reproved from behind. But I cannot go on, I have to look again.

He is there, he is definitely back. As if he had never moved.

Quickening my step, I retread the circuit of streets and after a shorter absence than before am back under my bush, above the house, looking at the black shadow beside the smithy.

Just in time. The tall figure has reappeared by his car, gigantic in the tricky light. For some seconds he stands, inspecting the vistas uphill and downhill, officially. But he is now off duty. The car door slams. The engine cries out, and with a breasting lift of the bonnet the car surges across the road and away down the hill, roaring again in the distance, a warning flung back into the sudden emptiness of the road. For a moment this emptiness is stupefying.

Then like a black cat taking its chance the watcher steps out of his shadow, crosses the road and jumps over the wall beside her gate.

Not to be outstripped, and aware that events have moved into a new gear, I walk quickly down the pavement, yet again, this time close to the wall of the gardens. I hear the dry creak of the door in the wattle fence. Has he gone through?

For a moment I stand. I have only one thought: What is this watcher and what is he up to?

The situation seems already so much my own, I have no thought of breaking free. How am I to get closer?

The faint fancy that she may yet this night be glad of my intrusion gives me a slight smile. But the fancy is in place, for that long thin white face is somewhere on the other side of that door and full of purpose. The memory of that face makes me reckless.

Avoiding the gate with its sounding latch, I slip over the low wall. I reach the door soundlessly, by walking on the garden soil beside the concrete path. Now, like setting a mousetrap, I ease the door open. I stare through the widening gap as if intensity enough could put out feelers to explore the corners of the back garden. I sidle through the gap and stand.

The wind bullying around the house is a help and gives me confidence, for a bowling dustbin lid would be in order. But how can I hope to hear him? His movements are certain to be as cautious as mine, and he may be far more expert. Keeping now to the concrete path, I stalk down the house side, touching the side door gingerly with my fingertips as I feel with my sodden soles for the surface of the path. I am now standing at the house corner.

Incredible! I hold the house where she moves, breathes, listens, is, and yet for fully five minutes have not given her a thought. But I can hear nothing, as I peer into the back garden darkness, nothing but the irregular wind, coming and going.

Has the rain stopped? Just about.

Perhaps he is just around the corner here, within inches of me, listening for me as tensely as I am listening for him. I leave the path, moving out sideways, intending to find the fence between this garden and the garden next door, if there is a fence, and so feel along that to the bottom of the garden. But between house and fence, treading in some sort of loose soil, I am suspended. I listen.

A sharp crack, a heavy weight on a thick stick, from the bottom of the garden, and over towards the middle. I ache with immobility, allowing time for him to recover from his fright. Gradually, moving only when a special press of wind covers me, I move down the side of the garden. Now twigs come against my knees, prickles: gooseberries or raspberries. I crouch slowly, and feel over the soft soil with my spread hands. Is this a path beside me? I did not seek it before, thinking it might be cindered. This is bare hard earth.

Taking a hint from my position, I creep forward on hands and knees, keeping my feet well raised off the earth behind me, all the while staring into the dark till I feel as if my whole head were one baffled eye. That, to my right, seems to be a bower of low trees, bare at this season, or it may be the frame of a rose arbour. Ahead, either a high rough hedge or a thicket. The sudden onsets of wind seem to confuse my sight and my thoughts, and I realize I can do no more till I have another clue. I decide to remain motionless. I am pleased with the stealth of my advance so far. The wind rummages among these bushes in such haphazard abandon, it will take all my attention to distinguish the human sounds from the elemental.

I wait. I listen. I would see more if I were on my feet.

Slowly I turn my head, pressing my cheek to my shoulder, rolling my eyes into the far corners, till I see the black mass of the house behind me.

Why is it without light? I had expected to see at least a bedroom window lit, however heavy the curtains. Has she gone into a dark house? Is she sitting in the dark?

For some seconds, I hold my position.

The double chime of the half-hour is torn to scraps by an assault of wind, and absorbed by the unmoved earth.

Now I ease the strains of my joints, re-ordering the stresses in preparation for rising to my feet. I want no cracking of the bone-articulations. I ease my whole position. Gradually I transfer weight from my hands to my knees and bring my left knee forward, setting the sole of my left foot to the earth. I am now almost in the starting attitude of a sprinter.

At this moment I freeze. It comes from behind me. It is incredible.

Clear, naked on my ear as if they took form in the very fibres of the nerve, softly popping flute notes!

I express my amazement by pulling a slow, skin-stretching grimace, a contorting leopard-mask, in the pitch darkness. I hold it, as the flute-notes play over my brain.

From behind me, immediately! Whoever is playing must be crouching there, smiling at me as he plays. He has watched my every move, for he has crept up with me step for step. He is playing his flute for the sheer idiocy of our situation.

Again, this time curving my body a little, I turn, slowly, because I may be wrong. I may be still undiscovered.

And I *was* wrong. How did I miss seeing him before? How has he missed seeing me? With his back to me, he is squatting on his heels, facing the house, his trilby bowed forward, moving slightly as the flute notes, in complete disregard for the wind, climb, step by step, step along, climb, step along, descend tossing something, plunge and search deeply over a dark floor, emerge, climb, climb, work at a height, flaking bright bits off . . .

The house is utterly dark.

I ease back, till I too am crouching on my heels, and I turn slowly, my whole concentration on the flute notes, for their first faltering, and on the brim of his trilby, for its first alertness. Now I could stretch forward and tap him on the shoulder. Gloating, I fumble on the earth for a stone, but all I can find is a twig, a forked nub of twig. Evidence! I pocket it. He does not know I am here.

And now in a kind of inane ecstasy, I writhe up my features again, stretching my mouth wide, making my eyes bulge, like a man laughing at tremendous volume or uttering a battle-cry, but in absolute and prolonged silence, while the flute notes dot and carry about the black garden and climb the wall and tap at the dark window and come circling back to the bowed attentive figure here, not three feet in front of me.

The Head

My wife is strange, I know. And living with such a strange woman, I have become strange too. But it can be explained.

Once upon a time my brother and I were hunters. We collected skins and heads and sold them to tourists who wanted to take a trophy home.

One year we heard that incredible quantities of game were assembling in the Three Heads country, at the mouth of the Sang River. At the right moment we set off, intending to kill all we could as usual.

The local Indians were the Slotts, a filthy, secretive pack of aboriginals mongrelized with various dirty whites, but fanatic hunters and first-class guides, and from them we wanted a guide. That's where we got the first warning.

They made it clear they didn't want to help us. After a deafening amount of gabble their chief stepped out, distinguished in no way, just as filthy and disreputable as the others, and told us what he didn't like about our request. We had come at the wrong moment, we were wanting to disrupt the forests and the animals at a great sacred moment, when all the animals were coming together to be counted by their Lord, and this was happening now. Though it happened only once in thirty years, we had picked the very week, the first quarter of this particular moon, and he the chief and his people forbade us to go any further.

We didn't believe his superstitious rubbish, but we were keen to get to the animals before they scattered again for whatever reason, and we surely needed a guide, so my brother produced something from our baggage. It was an Egyptian dagger. Its blade was cut and hammered from an old wartime fuel can, but its hilt was studded with fancy glass. We let the old chief examine this and he began to think.

So now he explained. He explained that it was impossible for a natural man to go into the forests at this time because the Lord of the animals would strike his body dead, rip his head off and skin it and leave it, or he would do the same to his spirit, kill his spirit and rip his spirit's head off and skin off its spirit skin and send him home again like that, absolutely mad and in anguish. But now he explained he could see that we were already mad and indifferent to fear and pain. He could see that we would go ahead and do as we liked. The Lord of the animals had no power over us. And he could give us a guide too, a man as mad as ourselves, or madder, who would be safe in the forests just the same.

Then the chief closed his hand round the Egyptian dagger and called out his madman. The man was not mad at all. He was simply half-witted. His name was Dazzled Falcon.

So we set off.

Now we had a new problem. Dazzled Falcon didn't want to guide us. He was half-witted but he didn't want to be mad and he didn't want to be struck dead by the Lord of the animals, so he started lying down on the trail. My brother lifted the safety catch off his rifle and set the muzzle on Dazzled Falcon's nose and threatened to make his head unskinnable, body and spirit. The wretched man got up crying and shaking his hands and clutching his head. He certainly was a pathetic creature. He looked like a bundle of old animal skins, badly cured and very smelly, with a big ugly ring made of two eagle claws through his septum and a dark wizened face like the smoke-dried head of a monkey and big round dark monkey eyes shiny with fear. He was soon terrified of my brother.

I was wary of my brother too. My brother was criminal to the bone. His eyes were flat and flickered too nimbly. His teeth were unnatural – just two bands of yellow ivory sawn with crude vertical saw cuts into rows of simple pegs, and he looked at you with his lips parted in a slight smile so you could see how the lower row closed in front of the upper.

I think he would have killed the guide quite easily and the guide knew it. So he wailed his sing-song gibberish and went on ahead of us, over the mossy rocks and fallen trees, under the thin late summer sunlight. It was strange to see him out there, picking his way, alone and pitiful, with great superstitious horrors in front of him and my brother's eyes and rifle behind him. He looked like a condemned man being driven to his execution somewhere in that vast mouldering of ancient forests.

We found the river, and suddenly the game was all round us. Every hundred yards it was bears, sitting on their backsides to watch our mules and investigate the procession of smells that came with us. When we glanced up, without fail a weepy-eyed cougar was gazing down. Or a lynx was angling his crested ears at us. When we glanced left, elk jerked their racks up, among the black trunks. When we glanced right, over undergrowth, the fleur-de-lys heads of deer flickered and went. Martens bounced from tree to tree among the high boughs, and wolverines bobbed over the roots. And all the way, open and bold, on either side of us, in relays, wolves kept pace like tame dogs, yawning and showing their back teeth. Whatever the Slotts thought about it, there had to be some explanation for all this. But we withheld our fire. We pressed on, planning to camp that evening and to start killing at dawn for skins and heads.

We pitched our tents at dusk, among bilberry bushes, between forest and river, and within sight of the northern sea. We were trembling with excitement. Mink ran over our feet as we unloaded the mules. The stony bare peaks round us lifted the long broad valley like a hammock, and all along the scrubby river meadows, and right up under the beards of the hanging forest, animals were moving. The air cooled. The first quarter moon was sucking up the last colours. Every twig and stone glowed like the body of a wild creature. The crash of leaping fish echoed among the conifers.

But it was an eerie land and with every darkening minute its power grew more awful. The mountains came closer. They leaned out over us, with a cold harshness that hurt our throats, and the river spoke with a dark tangled voice that filled our heads with voices. I felt the pressure of a great watchfulness. When we moved, we moved like thieves and whispered. I kept jerking round, to look behind me, but it was only an elk, twenty yards away, head up, or the lump of a bear, or a staring fox.

Dazzled Falcon had reached his limit. He huddled under a wall of rock, blubbering with misery like a punished child and picking apart a torn-up handful of forget-me-nots, and repeating over and over that he must not look at the mountains and he must not hear the river because they meant death. And he kept this up until my brother went across to him, and kicked the soles of his feet and ordered him to make a fire and shut up. Dazzled Falcon obediently shut up. But then he sank further over on his side, like a dog abasing itself, till the top of his head touched the ground, and he stayed like that, with his knees pulled up, and his hands still clasping the torn flowers, and his upside-down eyes tightly closed. And there we left him. After days of red meat we craved for fish. In the last gleam of silhouette light we stepped into the river and began killing fish.

We had wanted only one good fish. But now every fling of our lures connected with a walloping weight. We killed fish till the moon dropped behind the knife ridge and left us working by touch alone, and still the killing went on, and the gaffing and the clubbing, and the reaching out again into the blind voice of the river and its few smears of stars. The incredible plenty did it. We could not stop because we could not believe it.

At last like men waking out of a dream we climbed out of the river and stood erect, amazed at the darkness. We piled and counted our dead and heard again the balanced weight and stillness of the world, where the river trembled like a needle. We carried back one fish and roasted it. But Dazzled Falcon would not share it and would not sleep in the supply tent. And so we turned in and left him to the ember glow and the close-up circle of magnificent foxes that lay with their noses on their paws watching him in deep concentration and beyond them the coming and going lamps of many eyes.

At grey dawn he had vanished. Our speculations about him ended when we saw our pile of fish had gone too, eaten by bears. We could see eight bears working among the bilberries further upriver and eight shots expressed our fury and started the killing of the first day.

We used the mules to yank the skins off and left the naked human-looking corpses lying in a heap. A pack of thirty inquisitive wolves had assembled at this operation and without moving a step we massacred these, then skinned them warm and added their carcasses to the pile and called that place the Cemetery.

So the rest of that day we worked at killing and skinning as ditch diggers work at digging, with panting and sweat and growing aches. Far from frightening the game, our gunshots did not even make them nervous, but seemed actually to attract them, like some specially subtle and successful call. With minimum swing of the gunbarrel's angle, we emptied the magazines. We brought down clusters of bull elk to clear the aim to bigger clusters of bull elk. We moved three paces to align a cloud-blue cougar with a white wolf, threading both beasts with a single bullet. At one count I knocked down fourteen bears without lifting my cheek from the walnut or looking around for the next target. By noon we were selecting only the best specimens, but that hardly interrupted our fusillade. So until the sun went and the light blurred in the gunsights we slackened the rich pelts and shook the bodies out of them, without losing sight of our tents. At the day's end the rolled-up salted skins and sawn-off antlers were a pyramid well up the three pines round which we stacked them, the Cemetery was a terrible hill, and even the mules were exhausted.

We sprawled at our fire, stupefied with triumph, our shoulders numbed by fourteen hours work at the heavy rifles, our heads coked with gun crash, our atoms jolted loose, and visions of collapsing animals at every blink of our eyes.

We roasted grouse and remembered Dazzled Falcon. We invented theories for the uncanny tameness of the animals and their unnatural plenty, and for our guide's fear, and for his disappearance. Finally we fell back and slept, glutted with sensations of killing and skinning, our bodies weary as tattered rope, under stars that seemed to be dripping with abundance and life.

That night I dreamed this dream. Dazzled Falcon rushed into

our camp and he was skinned and bleeding. He tossed a cloak of white feathers like great Arctic owl wings as he kicked out our fire and scattered the embers. Then he bowed low over my sleeping brother and started to eat his face.

In my dream I sat up and shouted. The guide lifted his head and stared at me, then came very slowly towards me, so slowly I could observe in detail the lipless teeth and lidless skinned eyes and all the silvery blood-seamed glistenings of his flayed skull. Then he moved sharply, and struck out, and I felt it like a slap direct on the solid meat of my heart with the hard flat of a hand. It knocked the breath out of me. He went on staring at me, with those dreadful mutilated eyes, and backed slowly off, then suddenly he was bounding away over the moon-blanched landscape like a grinning wolverine.

I woke with a jolt and lay listening to a great commotion. It sounded as if hundreds of wolves were howling together, in every direction, near and far. And in among the wolves I heard another sound, like a woman shrieking. I identified a cougar. But as I listened each shriek dwindled away down into a sobbing so bitterly human that my hair and body froze. And I lay there like a lump of frozen iron as the din went on and on, till at last the shrieks seemed to climb and fade and again I was listening to wolves only. But soon they stopped too and night was empty of everything but the huge activity of the stars.

At dawn we stuffed ourselves with breakfast ready for a laborious day. I pondered my dream, but could see no point in it, so told my brother nothing. Even while we ate we killed and dark shapes flung up their heads and dropped out of sight into the waist-high mist.

I went upriver towards the sunrise and my brother went downriver towards the sea, both of us firing steadily. Wherever I killed I stuck a part-peeled willow or alder wand into the river bank, level with the body, to mark it for skinning.

It was now I realized I was killing without pleasure. I dawdled, peeling and embellishing the rods. A big wolf stepped from the trees and walked towards me. Aligning my sights on his face I suspended my decision to fire, experimentally. He kept on coming, gazing at me steadily. What a strange feeling that was, holding life and death so lightly balanced in the wolf's helpless face. For the first time I understood what it meant.

Suddenly I saw the land in intense clarity, microscopic. In front of me stood a man in a brown leather jacket, with the swift slide of the river behind him. I saw the gleaming coppery substance of his features. I saw the three bands of mingled colour in his iris, and felt the pressure of his rifle's aim on my face. Then I was myself again, and the wolf had come to a halt, ten paces away, ears up, tail high and waving very slightly.

I lowered the rifle and looked into the pale eyes of the wolf. It occurred to me that I was being looked at by a sage, one who knew how to live. Clearly this world belonged to him. I was overcome by a dreadful sense of paltriness and at the same time a weird jealousy. I struggled to rectify my ideas. I lifted the rifle and selected the place between the wolf's eyes, and slightly above, where the few long hairs which are said to belong to the devil spring out. After all, this was only a wolf, and how else was I to end our confrontation? So I fired and the wolf turned a somersault backwards, as if thrown away, like any creature shot through the head. I swung my rifle towards three other wolves that had come close to observe. With three shots I attempted to clear my head of all further entanglement. Instead, ejecting the last cartridge case, I found myself trembling with a faintness like exhaustion.

Was I simply tired? Only a moment ago I had felt peculiarly well, packed with steely energy. This was like the sudden shock of exhaustion of a wound. It even occurred to me that my brother had sneaked close and shot me, for some mad reason of his own, and I hadn't heard the report, and had not yet felt the high velocity bullet, which had probably gone clean through me.

I looked up. The sun had cleared its disc, the mist had lifted, the colours were opening and deepening. Far above, eagles floated out, and down around my feet bees were bumping into wet flowers. Three bears had come across the river and were shaking themselves dry, making fleeting rainbow haloes. The distant crack of my brother's rifle rolled up the valley herding its echoes. I raised my rifle and began to kill.

Our rifles continued their dreadful conversation across a widening gap until noon. But then quite suddenly, as at a command, I knew I had had enough. With relief, I decided on my final shot and brought down an elk with antlers the breadth of a lounge. The great beast lay with his nose in a clump of marigolds and his eye fixed with apparent interest on the vaporous blue peaks. It was over.

I sat down, heavy and dull. I watched the fleas crawling in the elk's ears. I decided that what I felt was the fatigue of yesterday and lay back and slept briefly and nightmarishly and awoke stiff, the sun hot on my sweating face. I thought of all the skinning to come and a deadly fright struck me, mingled with the glancing half-sleep dream of a physical blow. I actually had the impression that a skinned blood-soggy head struck my face, and I almost cried out. Then I remembered my dream and the painful slap. Had some venomous insect bitten me in the night? Was this a simple fever with a simple cause? I shifted my position so the elk could look at me with his dead brilliant eye in the hot sun.

I stumbled back to camp with vague limbs, the herbs and nectars exploding their perfumes under my tread, the sun rough and fiery on my nape. For yards at a time I walked asleep in muddled dreams, and kept waking with fresh surprise, seeing the rifle under my arm, and the blood-tinged sameness of the bilberry leaves or maybe the body of one of my victims, slumped in a heap of itself, arrested there in its few square feet of world, obedient to the law of bullet-holes, attended by grasses and flowers and insects, irreversibly dead in that beautiful appalling land.

My brother was already at the tents brewing coffee. After reviving me with a cup he told me he had found something he felt I ought to see for myself. He led away downriver. His manner was ominous but I was too exhausted and preoccupied to care. Then where the herbage ended and the estuary sand broadened towards the sea he stopped and pointed. I went on, walking out on to the sand, towards what looked like a dead merganser stuck on top of a stake in the sand a few yards above the waterline. I kept going, with the combined momentum of exhaustion and now curiosity. As I walked I was aware of the never-trodden ancient knives of the peaks, the bristly ridge of sea over the estuary bar, the purity of the sand, the twisting plunge of harpoon-shaped birds.

In that short distance I went on a great journey and returned, to find myself staring at a flayed human head, blue-silvery over skull and cheekbone, with bloody teeth and naked eyeballs, and a ring of two eagle's claws still clinging to what was left of the nose. Dazzled Falcon gazed into the sky behind me, without eyelids or lips or body, and his blood trickled blackly down the stake.

Then I saw a single track of prints of bare human feet that led up out of the shallow spill of incoming tide, across the sand, to the stake, ending at the stake. No prints came further and none went back. As if the head itself had walked to that place, out of the estuary, on bare feet, and planted itself there, and stayed.

Without a word we returned to camp and sat eating cold lumps of flesh and drinking coffee. My brother was staring hard at me. The blood-heavy head kept dipping itself into the hot liquid. When I proposed that savages, probably the Slotts, the guide's own people, had followed us and were watching us and had set up the head, as a joke, to indicate our fate to us, my brother laughed. Then he laughed again and stared at me, silent, and sipped. As I watched him the familiar thought came creeping back, that my brother was not properly human and that he kept up a show of being human only by great continuous effort of imitating the human beings round him. Then he laughed again, his hard excessive laugh, as if the laughter were scratching some unbearable itch deep inside him.

And at that moment I became afraid. It was suddenly quite clear to me who had beheaded Dazzled Falcon and skinned his head. My brother was getting up. He dropped his metal cup and I heard him saying: 'Now for some more skinning.'

My fever had come back worse. I knew I was approaching only a tiny black-rimmed circular view of what was going on. With effort I could expand this slightly. But it threatened to close altogether.

Working full out and using the mules we got the skins off all the dead animals, left the nudes where they lay, salted the skins using up the last of our salt, and rolled them up and stacked them, by late afternoon. Afterwards inside the tent I fumbled with the medicine chest and my brother stood across the light, gun under his arm, watching me and saying he would now kill for both of us. I said we had already killed too much. He said I must be mad and maybe this was what the chief of the Slotts had meant. I'd already lost my head somehow. I told him I never wanted to see another animal drop. He said no more and his shadow left the light. I heard the crack of his rifle, two hundred yards away.

I lay back and began to dream brief disaster dreams of animals. I was awake and hearing every repeated slam of my brother's rifle and its tumble of echoes as he moved up the valley. Nevertheless elk ate my feet. Bears skinned me with their claws. Cougars licked my bones to a bright whiteness. My brother became a half-witted wolf and attacked me. Then real wolves caught him and tried and sentenced and executed and ate him. But at last I slept.

I woke clear-headed but strengthless. I knew straightaway something hideous had happened to me. I lay in a slough of horror. I felt to be physically composed of dead eyeballs and dead teeth and coagulated blood. My whole being was saturated with animal wounds and animal pain and animal death. And the thought of killing one more animal wrenched me with agony like a hand grasping a raw burn.

I plunged out of the tent to escape myself but then stopped halfway as my eyes fastened magnetically on a tiny distinct black shape beside the dark hill of the Cemetery. I made out the shawled figure of a woman bowed low before our skinned victims as if before an altar. And as I watched I heard short tearing shrieks, one after another, three together. Then after a pause three more. At each shriek her body doubled up as if she were squeezing the sounds out of her stomach.

Then all at once she was moving and a shock of terror went through me. She moved swift as a running deer but erect and gliding smoothly over the rough scrubby terrain as if she were on a rail. She bowed again over the body of a bear, fresh-killed by my brother as he went out, and again I heard the shrieks. Then a sobbing, muttering, lamenting sound. Suddenly she was a hundred yards nearer, bowed over a pale scatter of freshly killed wolves. She had moved like a trout, disappearing at one point to reappear instantaneously at another. Then I saw the head jerk up and listen, as another shot crumbled across the valley in the still evening.

I wriggled under the back of the tent and ran crouching into the timber. When I looked back from behind trees she was already at the tent-door, her head up listening as two more shots came. Then her head ducked and she disappeared inside.

The sea breathed quietly. The peaks solidified as the light failed. The moon enlarged, lumpish and yellow overhead. The steep forests hung to the river meadows, like masses of freshly emerged insects with antennae quivering. The river tolled in its trench. The whole valley was like a vast listening conch.

And suddenly she was there, outside the door of the tent holding my rifle and looking straight towards me. I closed my eyes and imagined stones buried deep among roots in my efforts to disappear. I opened my eyes and she had come up close, within ten paces. I tried to make out what she looked like but the dusk was already thick. Her face was a deathly white oval. Her mouth was a round black hole. She seemed to be staring at me through her mouth. I waited for her to raise the rifle.

But already she had turned and in that immense hush and under those immense hanging mountains and with that unnatural gliding speed she moved away towards the river. I watched her go right down to the river. And I saw her go into the river and under the water and disappear, still carrying my rifle.

After a while I returned to the tents and lit a big fire and sat staring into the blaze, my whole brain stunned like a nail driven into a block of wood.

*

My brother came suddenly out of the darkness and sat down opposite me. He was breathing heavily and seemed to be in a frenzy of excitement. His face and beard were darkened and matted with blood, his hands and jacket glistened blackishly, and his eyes glittered. He kept groaning to himself like a man in some secret ecstasy. As he gulped coffee he began telling me about such killing as he had never dreamed possible. In four hours he had emptied seven boxes of cartridges, twenty-five cartridges to the box, and failed to kill outright on only one target. His appearance alarmed me. His brows arched, his eyes wide, as if some dreadful sight had fixed them like that. I remembered the photographs taken of infantry-men after battle. I remembered the cooling rooms for Chicago cattle slaughterers.

I listened, saying nothing, trying to make out whether he was mad and raving. He described the massacre of twenty jet-black wolves, beautiful fresh pelts for the morning and probably priceless. Evidently he had killed among twenty-eight bears five pure white ones, all big males, and in the way of coincidence five white cougars, a thing unheard of. And even this was only a beginning.

He went off into the dark and returned leading one of the mules heavily loaded. Then he threw down beside me a big loose pelt, wet fresh, the size of a bearskin, and challenged me to identify it. The texture was both familiar and strange. He told me it was reddish in good light, a foxy colour.

It baffled me. Then he laughed his laugh and unloaded a body from the mule, letting it collapse slackly to the ground. He rolled it into the firelight with his foot and I stood up.

What I saw in front of me was the flayed body of a giant human being.

No, he said quickly, it is not a man. Horrified and fascinated, I kneeled and looked closer, lifting the hands which he had not

148

skinned out, slender hands, twice as long as my own, furred like paws but bare-palmed. I saw the arrangement of the lines on the palms was human. Then I saw its sex in an oasis of unskinned hair, and looked up at the face sharply, but the lidless eyes and the lipless teeth of the skinned head confirmed nothing. He laughed and assured me it was not a woman either.

Then he told me it had come up out of the river, inside the forest. First he had thought it was a wild man. Then he knew he had discovered a new kind of ape.

There was nothing for him to do but kill it. There was no other kind of negotiation possible. It came on so purposefully, with its arms out wide, seven feet or so from tip to tip, he realized zoology was not the priority. He knew the incredible strength of even tiny little monkeys.

He put the first bullet into the V of its throat, which had no effect except the creature stopped, and fingered the hole and slowly opened its mouth. He put the second bullet into the open mouth which immediately closed.

It started walking towards him again, its arms out wide. So he put the third bullet into the first hole, the fourth bullet into the nipple of the left breast, and the fifth bullet into the centre of the brow, where the wrinkles make a V. These, he said, were the worst moments of his life, when he realized this creature was not going to go down and was not going to stop.

So he went on, putting bullets alternately into that throat wound and into the left nipple. And the strangest thing, he said, and he kept on repeating it, the strangest thing was the way it gazed at him all the time as it came on, with the strangest gazing expression in its eyes.

He stopped speaking and sat for a while silent, as he remembered. I stared at him and tried to imagine exactly what he had seen. Then he told how he went on firing, until the creature's right hand took hold of his rifle barrel and lifted it aside, quite gently, like a twig at face level. Then the great arms embraced him, powerfully but still gently, and all the time the brown eyes were gazing into his. They stood for a while like that until it began to cough, and suddenly blood gushed from its mouth on to his head and face, its arms relaxed and it slid down at his feet, still embracing his legs. And so it bowed there, with its head between his feet, and it died there, and the blood poured out over his feet.

He became silent and I gazed at the corpse. Then he dragged it away into the dark and came back and drank more coffee, saying nothing now. He brought a bear-skin from the cache and unrolled it and laid the strange ape-skin flesh to flesh with it, to share its salt, and rolled the two up together, then sat once more silent, watching the perky-legged sand-grouse carcasses spitting and sizzling on their sticks over the embers.

I knew now I could not tell him about our visitor. Instead, I told him again it was my last day of hunting. I had killed the last creature I would ever kill. And I had thrown my rifle into the river.

He supposed the guide's head had deranged me with superstitious fear. I answered him. Our quarrel developed quickly. I knew he was disturbed but I was stunned by his eruption. Within minutes he was almost out of control. It seemed to me the hidden hatred of a lifetime was being poured boiling over me. I set about packing my gear.

Then he began to laugh. As I rolled up my sleeping bag he fired into it, shouting: 'Missed, God-damnit!' He told me that from now on, as far as he was concerned, I was a two-legged, half-witted wolf, and if he caught me snooping around the camp after tomorrow he might well shoot me and skin me. That glimpse into my nightmare decided me. Then he put a bullet through one of my spare boots and laughed: 'Third time lucky!' I took a hatchet and torch and sleeping-bag and went into the timber.

Hours later I woke suddenly, remembering everything. I had the impression I had heard a scream. I lay, watching stars through the branches, and thinking about the shawled woman. The river talked near and noisily.

Another cry came from the camp. Guttural, almost words, it was my brother's voice. I took hatchet and torch, which I kept dark, and walked out from under the timber, till I saw the pallor of the tents. Bats dipped at my head and that was reassuring. Then from inside our tent came a long sound – half a groan, half a sigh. Maybe my brother was dreaming about the red ape. I returned to my sleeping-bag.

At dawn when I emerged to load my gear, I saw all the pelts had gone from under the three pines, our mules and horses had gone from their pickets, and my brother's bloody socks lay outside the tent, with his severed feet still in them.

Inside the tent, among quantities of blood, lay many splintered lumps of bone. After some difficult seconds, I understood my brother had been killed and devoured during the night.

I piled his dead fragments with our gear, and heaped stones over it, but could not find anything of his head, or his rifle.

Then I noticed that the land this morning was empty of animals. All the carcasses had gone too. The ape's carcass, and the bear where the woman had paused yesterday, and the wolves, were all gone. And the Cemetery was empty. I walked mystified on the blood-soaked blackened grass of the site. Every corpse had vanished as if it had got up and collected its skin and walked back into the forest. Nothing dead remained but those bits of my brother.

Then I knew I had to get out of that horrible land fast.

But as I moved I heard a shout, and I froze. It was my brother's voice. 'Wait,' he shouted. 'Wait for me.' And he called me by my boyhood nickname.

In a flash I had formed a theory of how the severed feet inside my brother's socks were not his, and how the blood and bone fragments inside the tent were not his, and I knew that our quarrel was over, and I turned. And in the middle of the empty cemetery ground I saw a skinned human head.

The eyes in the head moved and my brother's voice came out of its mouth, saying: 'Take me with you.'

It was his. The strange teeth were there as well as the voice. I picked him up, crying mechanically over and over: 'What has happened, what has happened?' But now the head's teeth were tight clenched, so that I wondered if my touch were painful to it. I cradled the thing in my arm, and began to walk.

So began the journey I shall not forget through the crisp forest. As the sun rose, the flies found my burden, and swarmed equally over both of us. The death horror soaked into me, and before long I felt like a walking corpse with two heads. I tried to open conversation with my brother, but he had lost interest in speech. His eyes had rolled up under his brow-bones, his jaws had slackened, and he was asleep.

After half an hour, brother or no brother, I laid the head gently down on pine needles, and walked softly away.

Within minutes, explosive screaming shouts started up behind me. I heard the shattering of the dead lower branches of conifers. Then I saw the head bounding across the forest floor towards me, and even as I turned uselessly to run it caught me up and closed its teeth on my heel.

I levered the jaws apart with a stick, wrapped the skull in my jacket and so resigned carried it for some miles, entering rougher sweatier going, clambering the steeps and thorny tangles beside the river, until I stopped to rest and to eat the remains of the fish we had roasted on the first night. The skull's eyes were back at centre and focussed on me. I offered the undershot teeth some fish and tried again to talk to the gruesome holes of the ears in the peeled bone, but the head was dead in everything but attention until I pretended to sleep. Then it rolled up its eyes and slept.

This time, stealthier than before, I got a good confident start before the vindictive shrieks began to ring through the trees behind me. I crossed the river twice, I forced through tearing hooked thickets where I thought no lidless eyes or skinless gums would dare to push themselves, but the head caught me at last and clamped its teeth on to the fleshy edge of my hand. Then the strength flowed out of me and I felt the black tremblings of despair.

I lurched along carelessly, letting its weight simply hang by the grip it had. Soon it relaxed and slipped down to my little finger but there it exerted new effort and locked itself in position on the bottom joint. Then it rolled up its eyes and slept with locked jaws, dangling from my numb finger.

Suddenly it began to dream. Its eyes flickered and jerked, grunts gargled in its cut pipes and its teeth ground on the bone of my finger. I yelled into its blood-plugged earhole to no effect. Finally, I swung it against a tree to stun it, or wake it up, and with a lock-jawed shout it bit clean through my finger-bone and dropped to the ground.

I fell on my knees with the pain, gasping for cold oxygen, watching the dead jaws chew slowly and thoughtfully and seem to swallow. I rolled the head over to see if my finger emerged from its throat-tube, but nothing came out except a squeeze of blackish blood, then all the muscles became as before, still and dead. I bandaged my stump with a strip of my shirt and lay for a while, recovering from the shock and devastation and trying to think of a way forward. The head flickered its eyes and now and again moaned softly. I told it I could no longer carry it and if it wanted to come it would have to make its own way, and so I set off walking and the head tumbled behind me like a puppy dog.

It was nearly dark when I smelt woodsmoke and heard the cries of the Slott village. At the same moment I saw a foxhole.

I rested near the foxhole, and ate again, and pretended to sleep, till the head slept. Once its eyes were well up under its brows, I slid it on fern leaves into the foxhole, and on down as far as I could reach, then rammed it in further with a dead bough, then jammed rocks in beside that, and earth, and so blocked the hole absolutely, and stamped the face of it flat, and walked on into the village alone.

The Slott chief greeted me with amusement. He led me to an empty hut, had blankets and food brought, then sat chuckling with a gang of his warriors, looking at my finger stump with great satisfaction, and asking after the health of my rifle and my mules, which seemed to be a great joke, and made me wonder again how Dazzled Falcon and my brother had died. In the middle of my evasions a howling enraged scream from the top of the village brought them all to their feet, and I realized that the head was out. More screams followed, then a storm of feet past the hut, and within seconds I was alone.

The uproar intensified with multiplying screams like a contagious hysteria, while I listened for that central deadliest scream to start aiming itself towards me. I made my way through the scattering panic of faces and the wails of women and children being smothered away inside huts, till I came to the concentration of manly shouts at the top of the village and found all the men leaping up and down and to and fro in fierce activity around a prone body. Then I saw the squat bird sitting on the body. The size of a big owl, it crouched with half-lifted wings hissing and screaming at the spear jabs. As I arrived it soared into the air and came whirling towards me with racking screams. Spears and clubs knocked it to the ground where it skittered about like a horrible firework, still trying to get at me through a rain of spear-thrusts and down-whacking clubs, screaming all the time from its wide-open human mouth. My brother's head had degenerated incredibly in two or three hours. It had short stubby wings and powerful looking eagle's feet, hairy and taloned. Suddenly it picked itself up and hurled away into the forest.

The chief was shouting furiously as the casualty was examined. Many hands grabbed me and marched me back into my hut. Three warriors sat down in front of the door and I was a prisoner. I lay flat on the blanket and thought about the poor fellow with his torn throat and chest, and listened to the faint screams which still came every few minutes from the depths of the forest. At each scream my hair and skin prickled afresh with electric fright. I could imagine the head halfway up some pine tree, its wings heaving, panting with its exertions, its bald skinless dome split with fresh hacks, its bulging probably damaged eyes glaring towards the village, its dreadful unnatural brain thinking about me.

Then the chief came in, with his warriors, carrying a heavy-bladed hook-ended bush-cutting knife. They held it in ceremonial fashion and I watched it carefully, expecting the worst. The chief spoke gravely and I remembered the paltry knife we had given him. He told me I was responsible for the head-bird demon, because I had violated the sacred assembly of the animals, and I was therefore responsible for its victim, who was now dead, since the head-bird had come looking for me, to deal justice, but had killed in error in the poor light. Therefore next evening when the head-bird returned, as without fail it would, I had to give satisfaction to both it and the dead man's spirit. I was to go out with the knife and meet the head-bird and destroy it or be destroyed.

I began to tell them they were mistaken, and there was nothing to fear, since it was my own brother's head and not a demon, but I stopped, hearing my insane words, and because it struck me suddenly that maybe my brother's teeth and voice were a demon's disguise, and finally I kept silent because I did not know what to think, and because the full reality of what was happening crushed all words out of me. I simply sat there horrified, with all my ideas shattered inside me like empty bottles in a bag.

The following evening at dusk, all the old people and women and children were sealed away inside the huts, and the warriors lit an immense fire of pine branches that cracked in the flames like rifles and sent huge sparks flooding upwards into the boil of red smoke. I stood there, feeling sentenced, watching the moon writhe and shrink and go brown in the smoke, hearing the warriors quarrelling over what to do with me. Some wanted to send me straight out into the forest. Others wanted to keep me till the head-bird appeared, so I wouldn't be sneaking off and leaving the village to the demon's thwarted fury. The debate was silenced by a scream of deafening volume that seemed to come right out of the smoke over our heads.

We waited, staring upwards and in every direction, hardly daring to move lest we miss the critical moment of attack. Then another scream came from the forest's edge, but before we could look that way another came from behind us, on the opposite side of the village. Either there were two, or the head-bird was moving like lightning. I remembered the way the shawled woman had moved, not so much moved as disappeared from one place and reappeared instantly in some other.

It was too much for the Slotts. The warriors began to yell that the screams were calling for me. The screams wanted me. The forest was screaming for me. Immediately everybody was yelling that the forest was screaming for me, and I was pushed out of the village with the long heavy knife in my hand. I looked back and saw them all clustered at the wall of fire, watching me. There was nothing for me to do but walk into the forest.

As I walked in among the trees I was thinking there were after all simple but natural explanations for the skull bird. Peculiar things happen among savages. Natural laws bend to their beliefs. The disasters of our expedition were of this kind. The Slotts had killed Dazzled Falcon simply enough. I left out the one-way footprints. Their evil-directed will had possessed bears to devour my brother. Their superstitious hysteria, excited by the murders, had materialized as a skinned head, in mimicry of Dazzled Falcon's which had been a real head. I was thinking this, and noting that I was out of the light of the fire, and probably free now to go on walking all night, and wondering what had become of the scream, when something struck me softly on the chest.

I stopped and got my knife ready. I was listening for wings, or the snapping of dead twigs low on conifers, but the forest just stood there in the pitch darkness, absolutely breathless from the roots upwards, like a cave full of stalagmites.

Suddenly right in my face the darkness screamed. I had the impression a face about a yard from me had screamed at me with all its strength. My response was to scream back, changing my scream to a roar, and slashing the weight of my knife through the place where the scream seemed to be, and leaping forward and kicking out. But my swipe made no contact and I tripped over roots and fell on my hands and knees. At the same time something cruelly hooked and sharp and energetic began to screw itself into my head. I tore it off and for a second held the familiar heavy grisly cold lump, but fearful of its teeth and talons I slammed it to the ground at my feet and brought down my blade like an axe.

I got something with a solid whack, but the only result was that two screams instead of one flew up, one right and one left, and came in at me from either side. I whirled and swung my knife at the screams and sometimes missed and sometimes I hit a wet solid lump like a flying turnip. Two screams became four and six and eight until I twisted about in a flock of attacking screams, while hooked things hit me all over and fastened to me and screwed their metals into me.

Then somehow I scrambled clear and was able to pause and get control of my breath. The screams seemed to have fallen full length and to be having difficulties. Also, they seemed to have assembled back into a single voice. I jumped forward and put in two or three almighty downward blows that would have brought the head off a bullock, right into the roots of the scream. Then again I stood back, feeling that I was beginning to win.

But now I realized the screams were no more than moans, and soft feminine moans at that. The agonizing thought hit me that some woman had been out there in the forest in the dark, probably undergoing some ritual separation from the village, and I had caught her with my blind reckless blows. I bent low and felt about over pine needles and roots and groaned aloud as my hands came to the naked slender body of a woman.

I picked her up and her moans stopped. I thought, she is dead. And I thought, nobody could have survived those cuts. I listened for a while, to hear her breathing and also to detect any new manoeuvres of the head-bird. Everything was silent and still, and the girl draped over my arm seemed as loose and lifeless as cloth.

I carried her back to the village, and it did not occur to me

that if she was dead this could be the second death I would
have to account for. I thought only that she might be alive, and
before anything else I must keep her alive.

As I stepped into the firelight the waiting warriors cried out
and scattered. They must have listened to my battle, and now
it seemed to them I was coming in with the demon's body. I
understood that and called to reassure them. And as I
examined the perfect body of the girl in the light of the flames,
and searched in vain for the slightest wound, the warriors
came back and stood around in a wide, solemn, staring circle,
while the great fire writhed its top and boomed like a waterfall.
Keeping well away, the chief shouted to me. The girl was not
theirs. It was plain to him that the head-bird had become a girl,
simply to save itself from my knife, because it knew I was crazy
and could no longer see what was real.

I studied the girl's face to find some sign of a demon nature,
and it was true she did not resemble the flat-faced Slotts,
though she looked Indian enough otherwise. I could only
think that she was a wandering stranger, she was from
elsewhere, and at the moment she was unconscious with
shock.

I could not leave her with the Slotts. I brought her home and
kept her. She is strong, quick and intelligent, but silent. She
has never learned to speak or to write. And that is what is
strange about her, that she keeps her secret and is silent. In the
end I married her and never hunted again.

And this is the strange wife I now have.